Dear Reader,

I wrote *Want Some Get Some* during the Los Angeles riots. After the Rodney King beating, L.A. was seething. Some people took that rage to the streets. Also during this time, another famous video was circulating around. Jayne Kennedy, the Halle Berry of her day, was an actress, model, and TV personality whose image was shattered after a videotape of her was leaked—the first "sex tape" in L.A. It was a devastating fall from grace, which ruined her career.

Trudy's character was inspired by Kennedy's ordeal. I wanted to create a female character who was viciously exploited by a salacious tape. How would it make her feel? What would she do to get back at her ex Lil Steve, who sells her image?

In *Want Some*, the first part of Trudy's story, Trudy is harrassed mercilessly after Lil Steve sells her explicit videotape. Joan, Trudy's jealous mother, tosses her "tramp" daughter into the street. When Tony offers Trudy a slot singing at Dee's, she finally feels alive, but this puts her in the path of hustlers and thieves. Working as a teller in Beverly Hills, Trudy schemes to rob the bank and plans to let Lil Steve take the fall. She romances Charles, a mail carrier she doesn't want but needs, until he agrees to her plan. But Charles has a hothead girlfriend, hell bent on revenge, who is gunning to catch Charles in the act. And now Trudy thinks Jimmy, her last romp before leaving town, may be a cold-blooded killer with no qualms about hurting girls. Their adrenalin-pumping attraction pushes Trudy into full panic, but she downplays this fact to her friends. And although she resents being compared to her mother, a conniving, man-stealing snob, this bank job requires Trudy to lie, steal, and cheat.

Can Trudy's hairdressing friend Vernita get her to see the danger in this bank-robbing scheme? Is getting even with Lil Steve worth risking their lives? Keep reading to find out how a simple robbery turns Trudy's life into vengeful, sex-fueled drama . . .

Also by Pam Ward

Want Some Get Some

Bad Girls Burn Slow

Published by Dafina Books

Get Some

PAM WARD

Kensington Publishing Corp.
kensingtonbooks.com

DAFINA BOOKS are published by

Kensington Publishing Corp.
119 West 40th Street
New York, NY 10018

All Kensington Titles, Imprints, and Distributed Lines are available at special quantity discounts for bulk purchases for sales promotions, premiums, fund-raising, and educational or institutional use. Special book excerpts or customized printings can also be created to fit specific needs. For details, write or phone the office of the Kensington special sales manager: Kensington Publishing Corp., 119 West 40th Street, New York, NY 10018, attn: Special Sales Department, Phone: 1-800-221-2647.

Dafina and the Dafina logo Reg. U.S. Pat. & TM Off.

ISBN-13: 978-1-61773-267-6
ISBN-10: 1-61773-267-2
First Kensington Mass Market Edition: July 2014

eISBN-13: 978-1-61773-357-4
eISBN-10: 1-61773-357-1
First Kensington Electronic Edition: July 2014

10 9 8 7 6 5 4 3 2 1

Printed in the United States of America

Acknowledgments

Much gratitude to: My wonderful, sassy mother, Bonnie Moore, who drove us around in a VW bus and taught me the meaning of *family;* my un-stoppable father, the architect, James Moore, who zoomed his 911 with zest (rest in peace, Daddy); my blood sisters, Linda and Lisa, whose cars died or blew up on freeways and who helped and hoorayed me in countless ways; my brother, Jimmy, whose ride always stays clean, thanks for all the raw material and always being there; my cousin Rachel who typed this from chicken scratch, we won't say how many cars she had; to all the rest of my family, especially my sweet Grandpa George who gave up driving at 90 but still has steam in his eyes.

To Michelle Clinton and Bob Flanagan of Be-yond Baroque Literary Arts Foundation; to Leonard Miropol's proofreading eyes; to Eso Won Books, the World Stage and Beyond: Wendy, Wanda, Vee, Nancy, Michael, FrancEye, Peter, El, AK, Merilene, Kamau, Watts Profits, Rafael Al-varado, SA Griffin and to Eric Priestley who peeped me some game; to Terry Wolverton and Heather Haley of the Woman's Building and to Guava Breasts: Michele Serros and Nancy Agabian; to Arvli who encouraged all my artistic

Acknowledgments

endeavors, to Rob Cohen of Caffeine; to my homegirls, Alane O'Rielly, Claudia Bracho, Jeannie Berrard and Francine Lescook; to my new son, Ryan, to Michi and Ron Sweeney and the entire Abrahams family.

To my amazingly tenacious agent, Stephanie Lee, who believed in me from day one; to Selena James at Kensington and to my editor Stacey Barney who put gasoline to this dream. And lastly, to my beautiful and brilliant daughters, Mari and Hana, wear your seatbelts and roar and to *mi amor*, Guy Abrahams, an Olympian who held my hand the whole way and showed me the road to true bliss.

Want some get some,
bad enough take some!

A schoolyard threat sung before a fight.

1

Trudy and Jimmy

Jimmy slammed on his brakes and hung his head out the car. "Get the fuck out the street, you broke muthafucka!"

A wino had stumbled out into oncoming traffic. He did a knee dance near the edge of the curb and just laughed.

"I can't stand them fools!" Jimmy said loudly at the man. "Raggedy-ass bums make me sick!" His twenty-inch rims lapped against the low curb. The bum had to leap to avoid the SUV's tires and fell feet first in the street. Grimacing, the bum cursed them as they drove by. Trudy lowered her eyes and studied her hands.

Jimmy turned off Crenshaw traveling west from Leimert Park and started the slow climb up the hills. Trudy watched as they rolled along through the Dons. Don Felipe. Don Miguel. This was all residential. Stucco homes with pools and well-cared-for lawns. Baldwin Hills was the Beverly Hills of black Los Angeles and was immaculately groomed compared to where she lived.

They pulled in front of a Spanish-style home with a beautifully tiled roof and stained glass windows.

Jimmy jumped out and opened her door.

"Who lives here?" she asked.

"I do. Come on in." Jimmy opened the heavily locked door and entered a six-digit security code on a small panel right inside the door. As soon as Trudy stepped in, dogs were barking like crazy. There was a loud, angry chorus of harsh, ferocious growls and claws scratching over wood doors. There was a banging sound, as a dog broke loose from the room. He viciously raced over to where Trudy stood.

"Prince, Prince, stop!" Jimmy yelled at the dog.

Prince was a large Rottweiler with a heavy, wet jaw. The dog paid Jimmy no mind at all. It bolted past him and went straight for Trudy's legs. It jumped at her and then shoved its snout inside her crotch, growling while showing fanged teeth. Trudy screamed wildly and dropped her purse to the floor.

"Prince! Got damn it, Prince, stop!" Jimmy cussed at the dog, socking its face with his fist. But the dog was too forceful. He darted back

2

and nuzzled right inside Trudy's thighs. Trudy screamed again, frozen in her tracks.

"Prince!" Jimmy hollered again, grabbing the dog by its black studded collar. He took a golf club out of the bag near the front door and beat the dog down. Beat it in the legs, the rump and the head. Beat it so bad it lay down on its back, whimpering with its hind legs pointing up toward the ceiling. Jimmy grabbed the dog's collar, dragging him across the smooth floor, shoving him in a room and slamming the door.

"Shit!" he said, wiping dog hairs from his suit. There was a small trail of blood on the marble.

"I told Lemont not to leave the animals in the house. Sorry about that, baby. You going to be all right?" Jimmy gently placed both hands on her shoulders. "I didn't mean to scare you like that."

Trudy felt that horrible old feeling of dread. Like someone was playing the black notes of a song. Her breathing became labored. She started to wheeze. She cupped her hand over her mouth and breathed her carbon dioxide back in. She hadn't told anyone about these panic attacks. Trudy's whole body felt woozy.

"What's wrong?" Jimmy asked, seeing her horrified face.

"Come on, girl. You'll feel better after you have something to eat."

Jimmy led her to a dining table elaborately set

3

with fine china and long-stemmed glasses. In the center was a beautiful bouquet of fresh flowers.

"Those are for you, songbird." Jimmy held her hand and Trudy managed a weak smile. She took a large gulp of her wine and fanned her face with her hand.

Breathe, she told herself. *Breathe deep and don't panic.*

"Look, baby, don't trip. Them dogs ain't nothing but protection. I been hating on dogs since I was seven."

Jimmy buttered his bread and took a huge bite. "I used to walk to the store for my mama to get eggs and junk. Used to be a German shepherd stayed locked inside a chain-link fence next to Grady's store. Me and Cabbage would toss Coke bottles over the fence and run. Man, that was fun. When them bottles would crash, that dog went mad. Dog lost his mind trying to get back at us. We messed with that hound every day. Growling and barking, tearing up the yard. Man, we both laughed till we cried." Jimmy wiped tears of laughter from the corner of his eyes.

"But one day Grady left that gate open." Jimmy stopped laughing and leaned up in his chair. "We couldn't tell 'cause it was one of them kind of gates that opened off to the side. When me and Cabbage threw the bottle that day, all we saw was molars and fur. Cabbage took off, but the dog got my jacket." Jimmy took off the cuff

link on his left sleeve and rolled it up. He showed
a thick, rough row of pale, jagged scars.

"We didn't have no doctor money, so mama
dipped a rag in some Dr. Tichnor's and kept it
covered, rubbing cocoa butter until the skin
grew back."

Jimmy dipped a large shrimp in the horseradish
and bit. "Ol' Grady never did find that dog."

Trudy sat quietly. She watched him chew his
food. His light brown eyes held her gaze until
she looked away. She scanned the huge room.
All the furniture was ornate. It looked like a lav-
ish hotel lobby.

"I see your eyes popping behind that wine.
You think I'm some kind of baller, huh?" Jimmy
laughed.

Trudy looked at Jimmy. She was beginning to
feel okay. "Stock market must be good, or do
you just have nice friends?"

Jimmy ignored her and poured more wine in
her glass. His eyes went stony. He stared out the
window. "You ask too many damn questions."

Trudy studied his hard face. He reminded her
of her mother. Cold-blooded eyes. A harsh, ice-
pick stare. An anger that was always right there.
The agonizing silences she endured during din-
ner. The awful slow chewing of food. Trudy had
become expert at judging Joan's moods. How
she got out of the car. How fast she washed her
hands. If she walked in yelling, "Why isn't there
any food on this stove?" Trudy would have holy

hell to pay. When her mother got mad there was no bad word she wouldn't use, but her all-time favorite was "slut." If your bed wasn't made, you were an ol' lazy slut. If the dishes weren't done, you were a filthy ol' slut. Anytime Mr. Hall said he couldn't come by, her mother flew into a rage. Trudy looked at Jimmy and smiled again. She was glad he didn't ask about her family.

"Come on," Jimmy said, tossing his napkin on his plate. "Let's go out for a ride."

It was five in the afternoon and Trudy had some packing to do. "I have to get home," Trudy said, standing up.

But Jimmy grabbed her hand like he hadn't heard and strolled back out to his car. He walked strong, like a man sure of where he was going. His head was held high. His feet moved with purpose. He walked like he owned the whole block.

"Do you have to leave now?" he asked, pressing her against the car, leaning her over his hood. "You got anything like this waiting for you at home?" Jimmy stretched her arms back against the hood. She felt vulnerable but could feel Jimmy's muscular body. It was a strange mix of fear and desire.

The only thing Trudy had waiting at home was a big, bulging stack of pink past-due bills and a sink brimming with dishes. But she wasn't any fool. This was a dangerous brother. But something about that was incredibly attractive. Her body fought hard against her good sense.

Every vein was yelling, "I want him to touch me. I want his big hands on my skin." His silky shirt revealed hard, chiseled abs, and his biceps stood out like grapefruit. It wasn't like she couldn't. She'd done it before. She'd gone home with Billy last month after knowing him for as long as one slow song, but Jimmy was different. Jimmy was rich. Rich boys were used to getting what they wanted. She had to make him wait. Make him beg for it first. Trudy could hear Pearl's voice in her head.

"Girl, you got to hold out, make 'em beg for it first. Let 'em sniff some bone before slicing 'em some meat!" Pearl had smacked her own ass for effect.

"You don't fuck no first date unless you a paid trick. Dick needs to be teased or it don't take you serious. You make him wait and a man starts thinking he's special. Thinks you saving it up just for him. Besides, you need to find out who some of these fools are before you lay down with 'em, chile! Men'll tell a whole gang of lies just to get in them panties. Once they drop, watch how fast they clam up," Pearl would say.

"I have to get home," Trudy said, pulling away. "I'll give you a call tomorrow."

But Jimmy was forceful. Even his eyes didn't blink. His hard body had her wedged over the car.

"Don't go yet. Come while I make this quick run. It'll only take a minute, I promise." Jimmy held her arms tight and would not let go. She wanted to say no but he was so damn aggressive. And when he kissed her, all down her throat and almost to her breasts, her body was winning the fight.

Jimmy stopped and pulled back before it got too far. "Let's go," he said, opening her door and letting her into his car.

Jimmy took her down Stocker, past the oil fields off LaBrea. Trudy watched the sad rigs slowly bend toward the ground, like an old field hand picking cotton. They turned and traveled west, until they hit Culver City. They pulled in front of this old-looking tract home. Some of the shingles had come off.

He knocked on the door for a real long time before someone turned on the porch light. A small face peeked out from the window.

A white man who looked like he was in his late fifties slowly opened the door. He stood firmly on the porch and didn't let Jimmy in. Even though the man smiled, he didn't look friendly. He looked like he was trying to explain something important. But Jimmy kept pressing, kept inching up until the older man called out to someone in the house.

A younger man, about Jimmy's age, appeared at the door. The older man disappeared into the back. The younger man looked like the older man's son. He wore big, baggy shorts and an oversized T-shirt. He wasn't wearing any shoes. Jimmy asked him something and the younger man shook his head. Now Jimmy was the one who smiled but didn't look happy. Jimmy stepped real close to the young man's body. Trudy could see something change in Jimmy. It was barely visible. It was more in his movements. He stood very close and was whispering something serious. The boy's movements changed too. His body seemed to stiffen, like a chill ran down through his bones.

Suddenly the father came out again. His face was as tight as a mason jar.

Without looking at Jimmy the older man opened his wallet. He peeled off some bills. He handed them to Jimmy. Jimmy stared at the bills until the man peeled off a few more. Jimmy smiled and put the money in his pocket. He patted the young boy on his back, turned around and came toward the car.

Trudy watched the man and son look toward her.

Jimmy jumped in and angrily backed out the car. He made a sharp U-turn, and the giant SUV felt like it might tip over.

Trudy sat silently in the passenger side. She felt stupid coming with him now. But there was nothing she could do.

Jimmy ran through a stop sign and drove dangerously close to the parked cars. He looked determined and never once looked at her. "I have to make one other stop."

Trudy shrank back as his tires dared another red light.

"Slow down, baby. What's the big rush?"

Jimmy sat staring straight ahead.

Trudy was getting more and more nervous. He had already run two reds and was edging someone else off the road. A yellow truck honked angrily at them as they passed.

Jimmy pulled up next to the man. He rolled down his window and screamed from the car, "You want some of this, you no-driving punk?" The truck driver quickly sped away.

Jimmy drove to a residential area in Beverly Hills. Trudy looked out the window. "Ah shit," she said to herself. It was the house of the tan-suit man she'd followed home from the bank. Jimmy leaned out and rang the buzzer until the metal gate slowly opened. Trudy scooted way down in the passenger seat. She didn't want the tan-suit man to see her face. She was glad when Jimmy didn't invite her in.

"I'll be right back," Jimmy said, closing the door hard.

But he wasn't. Jimmy was gone a long time.

Trudy sat in an orangey haze for almost an hour. And when the sun ducked behind a house and the street immediately turned gray, she yawned, putting her palm across her mouth. She was bored looking at the same manicured front yards and clicked opened the glove compartment and began rummaging inside. She saw a crumpled map and a pair of black gloves. She saw an envelope from the DMV. She pulled it out. It was the registration for the car. Trudy pulled the paper all the way out. The name on the outside of the envelope wasn't Jimmy's. The car was registered to somebody named Zeno. Then she saw a little black notebook. Trudy flipped it open. It was a list of deposit amounts and dates. She saw a flowered organizer shoved way in back. The organizer looked girly, like it belonged to a woman. Trudy pulled it out and unzipped both sides. Inside was a large metal gun. Trudy heard a door close and looked quickly up. Jimmy and the tan-suit man were closing the trunk of a Lexus. They lifted a tire and put something inside. Now Jimmy was coming. The tan-suit man came too.

Oh my God! Trudy thought. *He'll recognize me.* She zipped the flowered case but the zipper got stuck. She tugged at the zipper but it wouldn't go any more. She saw the tan-suit man at Jimmy's side. They both were almost at the black SUV's door. Finally the zipper broke through the snag and rolled around the case. Trudy shoved the case inside the glove box and shut the small door. She pulled on the seat latch until she lay completely flat. She peeked and saw

Jimmy two steps from the car. Trudy closed both her lids just before he opened the door, pulling her sweater up close to her face.

"What, you asleep?" Jimmy asked, shaking her a little too hard.

Trudy pretended to yawn and opened her eyes. Jimmy placed a small satchel behind his front seat.

"Let's roll." Jimmy wiped his nose a few times. He kept sniffing and talked fast but was driving even faster. He drove over toward Dee's Parlor, and along the way they passed Vernita's shop. Trudy thought about asking him to drop her off at Vernita's. But it was late. It was almost ten now and although Vernita was known to do a few heads after hours, nobody would be in her shop now. Trudy could see the metal row of hair dryers gleaming through the window like plastic jack-o'-lanterns.

"Girl, I feel like a million bucks next to you." Jimmy leaned over and rubbed his hand on her thigh. "So where do you stay?" Jimmy asked.

"I'm right down here. Turn left when you get to the end of this block." Trudy showed Jimmy where she really lived. She knew he'd find out if she didn't.

He pulled up in front, unlocked her latch and walked her to her front porch. It was nothing like Baxter, her in-between stash. Trudy saw him when the nights got too lonely. Baxter drove his daddy's old beat-up Voyager. Its hubcaps were just as pitted as Baxter's skin. When he dropped her off he'd lean across her lap and flip the latch for her to leave, stopped right in the middle of the street. He'd be gone before she stepped on the curb.

Jimmy grabbed her waist and pulled her to him. He kissed her like he couldn't get enough. On her mouth, on her cheek, sucking her lips.

Trudy was trapped in a mixture of pleasure and fear, panting like she couldn't catch her breath.

"So when can I see you again?" Jimmy asked. He had one foot on the step and his hand on the knob, like he was waiting for her to ask him in. But suddenly he stepped back and opened his wallet. He peeled off three bills and gently tucked them in her bra.

"What's that for?" Trudy asked, kissing him back. It was strange, but he flared up a daring kind of passion. Her good sense told her to put bars on the door but her body begged him to come in.

"I'm just paying you back," Jimmy said, stroking her braids, "for showing me a real good time." Jimmy kissed her slowly, rolling his tongue over hers.

Trudy cracked her door, easing it open slowly. She wanted him to come in. As her hands rubbed the muscles in his back, a moan escaped from his lungs. But Jimmy pulled away and turned toward his car. The next thing she knew he was back at his fender. "Girl, you going to have a hard time getting rid of me."

He waited until she was all the way in the house and Trudy flashed her porch lights like they were already tight.

When she got in, Trudy pulled the money from her bra. There were three fresh hundred-dollar bills.

"Well, I'll say," she said out loud to herself. This was the first time a man had given Trudy money. Her mother could always pull change from Mr. Hall. She worked Hall like a damn ATM machine. She'd sit in his lap, whisper in his ear with her tongue. Begging for small things she wanted.

Suddenly she heard a sharp rap at her door. She tiptoed to see. Her breath became labored. Was this Jimmy again? Did Jimmy suspect her already? She edged toward the peephole and stared through the slot. It was the landlord. He looked like he was about to use his key.

"Yes?" Trudy said. "What do you want?"

"Your rent's three weeks late! I need to get paid." The man stroked his beard. His hands were in his pockets. "Unless you want to make other arrangements."

Trudy didn't have her rent but she opened the door. She offered one of the hundreds to the man. "Will this hold you until next Friday?" she asked.

Today was Monday; that gave her less than five days.

The man's eyes rolled up and down Trudy's body. He loved his new tenant. He watched her every day from his porch. She was better than anything he saw on TV.

"Sure, that'll hold me. Uh-huh, Friday'll be fine." The man took a long time leaving her door.

Friday is fine, Trudy said to herself. She planned to be long gone by then.

Trudy unfolded one of the hundreds, smoothing it all out. She took out some scissors and a stack of newspapers. She held down the bill and traced around the edge, then began cutting up newspaper to the same size and shape.

She noticed the red light flickering on her machine and pushed Play.

"Trudy, it's Vernita. Me and Lil Steve's straight. Hit a sista back, you ol' stayin'-out-late hootch." Click.

"Hey, bootylicious! I got your number from Tony. Call me if you want some good dick." Laughter, click.

"Hi, Trudy. This is Charles. I've been thinking about what you said. Call me when you get this message." Click.

Trudy picked up the phone and dialed Charles's number.

"Hey, Trudy," Charles said. His voice sounded

nervous and low. "I was wondering if we could get together and . . . ah . . . ah, talk?" His eyes darted around the room for Flo. He could see her reflection in the large bedroom mirror. Flo was rolling her hair.

"We have to meet tomorrow," Trudy said quickly. She looked at the newspapers covering her floor. "Why don't I come over there?"

"Here?" Charles hadn't planned on Trudy coming to his house. He lowered his voice to make sure Flo couldn't hear him.

"You want to meet *here*?" Charles put his hand around the mouth of the phone.

"I wish you could come here but my place is being sprayed." Trudy's floor was littered with newspaper shreds. "I'm going to be gone for three days." Trudy used her slow, husky voice while she lied. "I don't know, baby. Maybe it's me. But I felt something deep that night when we talked. It's crazy but I've been thinking about you all day." She could almost feel Charles swell through the phone.

"Yeah, I have been doing a lot of thinking too." Charles watched Flo put the rollers in her hair. The upstairs neighbors sounded like they were pushing furniture across the floor. "Come on over. Tomorrow is fine."

Trudy hung up the phone and took a long, nice, warm bath. While lying on her bed, she smelled a hint of male fragrance. Picking up her blouse from the floor, she brought her sleeve to her face and took a deep, strong whiff. Yeah, that was it, masculine and clean. It was the wonderful scent of Jimmy's cologne. He was right in her shirt, lodged there in her sleeve. Trudy dropped the whole blouse over her face, inhaling the deep male scent while laying in bed. She dreamed of him holding her and gently touching her face. She looked like a child, rubbing the silk against her cheek, and even though she had orange nail polish on, Trudy started sucking her thumb.

Trudy opened all the windows in her apartment. Whenever she got panicky she got hungry. She placed a thick slice of chocolate cake on a napkin and took the piece with her to bed.

She thought about the dog growling low in her crotch and that man and his son looking scared on the porch, and the long time she waited all alone in the car and the long, knowing smile of her landlord. But mostly she thought about wild, hungry sex and touching Jimmy's rock-hard biceps again.

Suddenly Pearl's voice came into her head. "It takes a smart woman to pick a good man. Don't be dumb, honey. Life can be short. You could lose your whole life picking wrong."

But Trudy had her plan and was well on her way. She knew Jimmy and the tan-suit man were connected and that the Lexus was carrying a really big stash. Trudy inhaled the sleeve deeply. She wanted Jimmy. He could be her last taste of L.A. before leaving. So what if he had a slightly dangerous side. Who didn't? He hadn't done anything to her. She was already used to maneuvering herself around men. She'd handle him just like she handled her mother. She wouldn't be here long. She was leaving town soon. He'd be her last juicy swig before Vegas.

I'll be careful, she thought. *Look out for signs. Won't be nobody's fool.*

But see, that was the funniest thing about fools. They were always willing to be fools again.

2

Tony and Lil Steve

Everybody's got needs. Everybody's got wants. Lil Steve's was like hunger. Like going days without food. He could always feel that tight, awful pull under his shirt.

While Trudy was sleeping and dreaming of Jimmy, Lil Steve wandered the street in the dimly lit moon. It was one of those huge orange-hued moons, hanging so low you could touch it, like a flat pancake sopping in butter. He moved easily down the street. He passed the blurred neon of Dee's Parlor. He unrolled a bag and popped open a forty, taking huge swigs as he moved. He was almost there now. He downed the whole can and left it on top of a mailbox. There it was. The house he grew up in. Right down the street from Dee's Parlor. The grass was overgrown and the paint job was trying its best to hang on, but it still looked pretty much the same. The fig trees were there and the jasmine bush, too, and the low hedge he used to jump over.

No matter how late it was, Lil Steve would wind up walking or driving past his old house. Something kept pulling him back down this street, even though he hadn't lived there in years.

This was her house. It belonged to his mother. He remembered the steak, and heaping plates of steamed cabbage, and those warm, sudsy baths in the green tiled bathroom. But that was way back, when they all lived together. Before Daddy left for work and never came back and his mama hadn't learned how to drink.

Something changed in Lil Steve once his daddy was gone. Nothing he could put his finger on, but the change was still there. He didn't care much for school or model airplanes anymore. He just hung from his windowsill night after night, watching folks go into Dee's Parlor. He liked seeing the men in their nice shiny cars. Dudes with good clothes and nice rides and plenty of money, holding fine chicks with Jolly Roger smiles.

See, Lil Steve's mama had stopped smiling a long time ago.

"Heathens," she'd say, sweeping away at her porch. She'd suck her tongue hard at the short-skirted women, slam the screen door if a man tipped his hat. But as time passed, she'd stop and watch those folks too. The next thing Lil Steve knew, she was coming home late and the jasmine that stayed in her hair all the time was replaced with the foul smell of cigarette smoke and her breath held the tense scent of gin.

Lil Steve watched the house for a real long time. He looked in the window. The kitchen light was on and the front room glowed blue, and the TV blared from the barred metal door. Earl never could hear good. Lil Steve saw his foot. It was flung over the couch and his snoring oozed through the windows. He remembered when Earl had put the metal door up. How he covered all the windows with cold steel bars and the pretty yellow curtains that blew in the wind were replaced with the black grid of metal.

Lil Steve kicked a rock and moved farther down the street.

His mother thought Lil Steve had just messed up his life. She couldn't understand why all his good friends were hoodlums and thieves. Why he spent all his time in the streets. But his homies were the only ones he could really count on. The only ones who ever stayed loyal. Ray Ray was never gonna not be his boy. They had stolen lawn mowers and cars and had grown up out there together. He was the only one Lil Steve trusted. Besides, the people in the street were all just like him. Nobody had shit. Nobody was nothing. All of 'em hustlin', just trying to get over.

There was only one time Lil Steve felt like something. Only one person who could make him drop his cold-blooded guard. Make him look at life serious or lay back and laugh mighty. That was the short time that he was with Trudy.

Lil Steve kicked the rock farther down the dark street.

Yeah, Trudy was the best, and Lil Steve had had plenty. She was pretty and smart, with a criminal streak, and she treated him like he was special. But Lil Steve had fucked that up, like most things in his life.

"Besides, she'd have left me," Lil Steve said out loud. "She'da drop-kicked my ass once she saw I was nothing."

He picked up the rock and threw it up at the moon. Lil Steve lied to everyone he knew about Trudy. He called her lazy and fat and ugly and cheap. He couldn't bear thinking of her with anyone else.

"Yeah, she'd have left me. I'm damn sure of that." He opened the white pack and shook out a Salem. "Eventually, most women do."

A crow flew from one of the juniper trees, shaking tiny dead leaves to the ground. The sound startled Lil Steve and he crossed the street toward Dee's. The neon lights shone even when it was closed. He sunk his hands deep inside his front pockets and kicked a glass bottle across the street.

He gave Ray Ray a pound when he got to the door. Tony was inside wiping down the bar. It was well after one in the morning now, and Dee's would be closed in an hour.

"What are you doing in here?" Tony asked.

Lil Steve lifted his pant leg and pulled a fresh hundred from his sock. He handed it to Tony. He'd just gotten that bill from Vernita the night before. Now he and Tony were straight. Even if he couldn't gamble upstairs anymore, maybe Tony would let him come in for a drink.

"All right. Okay. Can I get you a beer?" Tony put the hundred in his pocket.

"Yeah, man," Lil Steve said, putting the beer to his lips. "We want to talk to you about the fight next Friday. You taking the odds for Liston?"

"You know I got the odds on anybody fighting these days." Tony looked at Ray Ray real close. He was standing there shifting nervously back and forth on each foot.

"What's up brotherman? You gotta take a leak or something?"

"Naw, man, but we do need to talk. I wanted to know if you had my check." Ray Ray avoided looking in Tony's eyes. He didn't want him to see how bad he needed the money.

"Your check? Nigga's always wanting to get paid. You lucky I gave you a fuckin' job, boy!"

23

Tony kept rubbing the bar. He didn't look up either. "You'll get paid when I say. Didn't I tell you that already? You about to piss me off out of a job." Tony waited. He wanted to see Ray Ray's reaction. Percy watched Ray Ray close under his dark tinted shades. Ray Ray gritted his teeth but he didn't move, and Tony chuckled out loud to himself.

Lil Steve stepped up this time. "Is it cool to talk, man? Are you busy right now?"

Tony threw down the towel; he filled an iced glass with gin. He smiled at Ray Ray but not Lil Steve. "Yeah, it's cool. Y'all come on upstairs."

Next to the gambling room upstairs was a tiny separate space where a couple of folding chairs kneeled against a wall and a leather chair peeked from a desk. Tony led them up the narrow wood staircase near the back. The stairs moaned and creaked under his weight.

Ray Ray and Lil Steve stood in the room. A hanging bulb swung over the ceiling.

Tony pulled the chain. He looked right into Lil Steve's face. "So how can I help you, Mr. Slick?"

Tony never liked Lil Steve. He had seen him take one too many card games, and some of the regulars claimed he had a system, but Tony hadn't figured the 411 on that yet. He watched him, though. Watched that ready smile and smooth handshake. Yeah, he was watching him steady.

"Why don't you boys sit down, take a load off your feet?"

Tony jammed his body into a ripped leather chair. He put one of his feet on the desk.

"What can I do you for, Ray Ray? You look like a hound that hasn't found the right tree to piss on yet." He cracked up at his own joke and slapped Ray Ray's back. Ray Ray shrugged his hand off his shoulder.

"Listen, Tony, we want a cut on some of the odds on Jones," Lil Steve said.

"Oh yeah?" Tony said, raising one eyebrow. He took out his red pack of Winstons and lit one up.

"And what makes you boys think y'all can get in? That's a man's game, son. You got to have more than a few chips. I'm talking double digits, boy."

Lil Steve stepped forward. Tony didn't mean shit to him.

"Look, Tony, I know you got this card thang, and it's cool. You the man. I'll give you that, but who can we talk to about fronting some long money on this fight you got coming this Friday?"

Lil Steve was smooth. He knew Tony didn't trust him. He had to come correct. That's why he paid Tony up front, as soon as he came in. He had to pretend to give Tony his props. Respect in the hood was all some brothers had. But it was hard for Lil Steve. The hardest thing he ever did in life. See, Lil Steve couldn't stand Tony's pasty black ass, after what had happened that night to his mother.

Lil Steve didn't know the whole story. But the parts he did know were hard. All he knew was his dad had left, and his mama took it bad. She used to wait every day for Lil Steve's father to return. She'd wait until sunset, until the streetlights came on, sitting on her front steps watching Dee's neon lights burn the sidewalk. After Lil Steve went to sleep his mother would watch Dee's doors. She hated the club but didn't mind watching all the people go by, like a child does a carnival ride. Tony would always wave for her to come over, but his mother always shook her head no.

Well, one night Lil Steve's mother was watering the lawn and Tony crossed the street with a drink in his hand. He'd garnished the rim with pineapples and cherries; a green monkey held an umbrella. Tony winked at her and left the tall drink by her screen. His mother waited for Tony to get all the way back inside Dee's before she picked up the drink and took a sip. The liquid was sweet but it burned going down, so she spit the drink out and splashed the rest across the grass. But she saved the small monkey and fingered the umbrella while looking at Dee's from her porch. And one long, lonely night after twisting in the sheets and biting her pillow, she bolted straight up, knocking her water glass to the floor. She smeared on her lipstick and crossed the dark street toward Dee's.

Tony had two old-time hard-drinking friends. One was an out-of-work drunk named Stan and the other was a jackleg mechanic named Earl. They were the kind of men who preyed upon middle-aged women. Women with pensions and old, roomy homes. Places they could live free and eat.

Earl started coming over and forgot how to leave. Like a mouse you couldn't get out your house. His mother acted different whenever Earl was around. She fawned over him. She spoke high-pitched and phony. Laughing too loud when stuff wasn't funny. Wearing extra makeup and heavy perfume. Saying all the time, "Earl, you kill me."

Lil Steve couldn't see what she saw in that fool, but the next thing he knew they were married. Ol' nasty Earl with his mechanic fingernails that were permanently black and that large retarded daughter of his. The first thing Earl did was put bars on the windows. He killed the front lawn with the gasoline jugs and dented car parts he stacked all over their grass.

But the worst was when his mother gave that retarded girl his room. Just gave it away like he was nothing. Made Lil Steve sleep on the couch.

Lil Steve tried his best to make his bad feelings heard. He stared Earl down, flashed him cold, evil eyes, calling Earl "son" even though Earl was thirty-nine years older, anything to make Earl mad. But Earl didn't care. He just laughed all the time. All he wanted to do was play dominoes or checkers or drink with his buddies. Yelling for Lil Steve's mother to bring his greasy ass a beer. Like his sloppy ass ruled the whole house.

In one swig his mama wasn't his anymore. The family life he'd known was a memory now. It had slipped through the cracks like a black row of ants. His mother stayed so busy with cooking or cleaning or drawing the girl a bath. Earl and the large girl both lounged around all day while his mama waited on them hand and foot like a slave.

He couldn't understand why she gave them so much. Why she sacrificed her life for two total strangers, just so she could say she had her *a man.*

One day Lil Steve just asked her point-blank, "Why you let that ignorant nigga pimp you like this?"

His mother stood there with both hands on her hips. "Boy, a woman has needs, a woman has wants. There are some things you can't understand."

Lil Steve couldn't stand watching her act so damn stupid, so he packed up and moved into his car. It was just after high school, so not many of his friends knew. He parked that car all over, traveling all over town, from Crenshaw to Compton, to Venice Beach or Pacoima, staying with anyone who'd feed or let him crash on the couch. He kept a gym membership so he had a place to shower and keep clean or to park for long hours without worrying about all those signs saying NO STOPPING.

But the simmering hate and street life scorched his heart. He started smoking crack to black out his brain. He started hustling full time to make money to eat. When his money ran low he broke up with Trudy and sold her nude video for cash. After that, he only dated honeys with money. He didn't like it but it gave him time to spy on his mother. Make sure she was all right.

But as much as Lil Steve hated Earl, he hated Tony more. He blamed him for what happened last summer to his mother. But Lil Steve didn't even know the worst part of the story. If he did, Tony wouldn't be breathing today.

See, last summer, Lil Steve's mother had gone over to Dee's. She was looking for Earl, who was having trouble finding his way home lately.

Tony blocked her path when she got to the door.

"Hey, girl, how you doin'?" he said, leading her away from the giant black gate that led to the gambling room upstairs. "Come on, have a quick drink on me."

Tony was always trying to get Lil Steve's mother to drink. He always stayed after her about it.

"Come on, sugar, it won't hurt you none. It's real nice and sweet. Guar-an-teed to make all pain go away." Tony poured her a white creamy piña colada, garnishing it with a dead-looking pineapple wedge.

"Now, Earl ain't doing nothing but gamblin' some. A man's got to do what a man's got to do. You don't want to chase him away." Tony knew about Lil Steve's father leaving. He knew where to put in the knife.

As the night wore on, the liquor set in. His mother started to sway back and forth in her chair. The warm room was beginning to spin.

"Come over here, girl. Give ol' Tony a kiss." Tony circled her waist with one of his arms. His other hand rested over her knee.

"Earl don't want me," Lil Steve's mother slurred.

Tony slid another drink in front of her face. "Pretty as you is, that's hard to believe." Tony let his hand roam farther up her thigh. "Shoot, I bet every man in here wants you."

"I know I do." Tony's friend Stan laughed. He was holding his fifth whiskey, sitting on her left side. Lil Steve's mother's breast kept grazing his elbow. He was having himself a grand time. But when he noticed Tony's hand creeping up her thigh, Stan started feeling uneasy.

She smiled and rolled back into Tony's warm arms. "Where's Earl? Did you tell him I'm over here waitin'?" She almost fell from her chair.

"Whoa," Tony said, sliding her back up. "Girl, let's get you some fresh air."

Tony stood up. He started to guide her outside.

But Stan stood up too.

"Man, don't mess with her. Can't you see she's sick?"

"So? What difference does it make?"

Stan's lip began to tremble. He struggled to get the words out. "That's Earl's woman, man." Stan said the words low. He hated to contradict Tony.

"Listen," Tony said, taking a step back toward the bar, "you like that drink?"

"Yeah."

"Whiskey taste okay?"

"Uh-huh."

Tony handed Stan the whole bottle but didn't let go. He leaned right inside Stan's wrecked, plastered face. "Then sit down and shut the fuck up."

Sweat began to drip from Stan's desperate brow. He worriedly glanced at Lil Steve's mother. She was swaying back and forth under Tony's whale arm. She had a tormented look on her clean, pretty face, like a puppy about to be gassed at the pound. But Stan was a drunk. His right knee was shaking. He couldn't pass up a free liquor bottle like this. He grabbed at the bottle but Tony snatched it away. Stan's sorrowful eyes pleaded. His mouth started to water. His shaking hands reached for the bottle again. Tony slammed it down hard on the table.

"You got something else to say?" Tony asked him again.

"Uh-uh," Stan said, sitting back at the bar.

Stan never looked back. He drank heavily that night. He drained the whole bottle and kept his bloodshot eyes glued to his glass.

Out back from Dee's was a cluster of trees. A mountain of cardboard boxes hid an old, beat-up mattress. Tony would sometimes sneak lonely drunk women back there. The old mattress reeked of cheap booze. There was a cat laying at the mattress's frayed edge, Tony kicked the cat with his boot.

He laid her down gently. He lifted her dress.

"Wait, Tony. Sto——op it. What we doing out here?" Lil Steve's mother squirmed but she was too drunk to move.

"Earl may not want you," Tony's gut straddled her body, "but I been wanting you for months."

Lil Steve's mother struggled, but the liquor had made her weak.

Her twisting body got Tony more excited. He stuck his tongue out and licked her whole cheek. She squirmed underneath him, but his giant girth held her firm. Tony's sandpaper tongue slid inside her mouth. The whole world spun fast. She felt dizzy and sick. All the trees began to fly past her eyes.

Earl found her later, passed out on the mattress. He didn't know what had happened and tried to wake her up, but she wouldn't budge. He poured the rest of his beer in her face.

Lil Steve was on his way home to his mother's house that night. He was only a mile and a half away.

Earl and Lil Steve's mother stumbled out into the street from Dee's bar. Earl was walking way ahead of his mother. She was trying to keep up, teetering on spiky black heels. Her dress was a mess. Her hair was on end. She was arguing with Earl and he was waving her away. She suddenly stopped and got sick on the lawn. Earl got in his car, slamming the door hard, and she got in, slamming hers too.

Now, Tony swore up and down she was driving that night, but Tony was damn good at lying for his friends, especially when they were running from their wives.

Earl and Lil Steve's mother used to fight in the car in front of their house so his big lazy daughter couldn't hear. Fussing until way after midnight sometimes. But this time, Earl revved the car's engine. He backed out the driveway, crushing the hedge on their front lawn, gunning down the street like some nut.

Everybody living heard that hard, deadly crash. The wild screech of brakes. The crashing of glass. The horrible twisting of metal. Folks rushed out their homes in house robes and socks. They came out of Dee's Parlor in droves.

Lil Steve heard the crash too as he skidded around the corner. He jumped from his car, leaving the door open, and ran right up to the wreck. When he got there, the car was completely turned over. The passenger side was horribly smashed. The whole front window was gone. His mother had been tossed straight through the windshield. Glass was all over her arms and her legs. Earl stumbled out and cried on the curb, drooling like some idiot boy.

Tony lit a Winston and sized up the damage. "What a waste of a Regal," he said, blowing out his smoke. "Shoulda bought that bitch when I had the chance."

And that's how Earl got Lil Steve's house. Everything his mama owned was all Earl's now, and there was talk going around that his big retarded daughter wasn't no real daughter at all.

It gnawed on Lil Steve awful to see Earl living in his house. It made all his insides bleed and feel raw. He struggled each day to not bash someone's head. To not pick something up and smash it back down. To just rip up something to shreds. He bit his own fist just to shift off the pain. But nothing made it go away. Sometimes he did shit to just mess with Earl's mind. He'd dump out their trash, spread it over the lawn, or let out the air in all of his tires, steal his rims or take off his gas cap. Sometimes he'd just pee on their grass. But whatever he did, Earl was always unfazed. When Lil Steve dumped the trash, Earl left the trash there. When his hubcaps were gone Earl didn't replace them, and he stuffed an old rag in his tank for a cap.

Lil Steve's only satisfaction came from cheating Tony out of his money. He used every card-playing trick to break Tony's bank. He hated his smug face and nicotine breath. How he dogged out Miss Dee and stole her club and her money. But nothing was worse than how Tony did his mother. Lil Steve knew some, but not the worst parts. If Tony hadn't given his mother her first drink, she'd still be alive. He could barely stand to look at him now.

"See, my man here will have five Gs on Friday," Lil Steve went on coolly. After the bank job this Friday they'd have plenty of money. "We have an anonymous investor." He smiled at that statement. They all did. Tony was listening. He didn't mind where folks got their Ben Franklins, as long as they could be recognized at the bank.

"We just want to place a little wager. Everybody saying Jones is going to take him in the seventh."

"You can have Liston to win or Jones if he goes eight." Tony took a small pad from his coat pocket, scribbled on it and tore the sheet off. "So where's the money at, boy?" Tony asked.

"We don't have access to all the funds now. We'll have it all to you by Friday." Lil Steve glanced at Ray Ray and back at Tony again.

Tony took a long drag and smashed it out in the ashtray. He'd heard so much yin-yang about money, he could hardly keep track. He smiled at the young junior flips and stood up. "Yeah, well, until you get your investor together, don't come in here and waste my damn time." He crumpled the paper and tossed it in the trash.

Big Percy came upstairs and followed Lil Steve down.

"You boys need anything else?" Tony asked, waiting.

"No, man, we cool. We'll be back." Lil Steve nodded.

"What them fools want?" Percy asked Tony when they walked out.

"Just some young-ass bullshit. I don't know, hell. Probably be calling someone's mama tonight to bail their punk asses out."

3

Tony and Flo

Tony walked to the kitchen and spit in the sink. His buddies Earl and Stan were sitting at a card table in the living room. It was afternoon, when the club wasn't open yet; Tony liked to play cards at home with his friends.

"Probably serving that skinny nigga right now," Earl yelled to Tony. Earl loved instigating shit.

He sneaked himself a quick shot of gin while Tony was in the kitchen and drank it down before Tony came back.

"Charles, you know that fool, the one who took Tony's woman. They say he owes Tony a whole bunch of money." Stan snuck himself another quick shot too and poured more in the flask he kept inside his jacket.

Tony stumbled back into the living room, where the other two men sat at a tiny card table.

"I saw Flo," Tony told his old drinking buddies.

Earl and Stan nodded their heads. They'd heard this sob story so many times, but they never complained. They always agreed with everything Tony said. The drinking was free, the ham sandwiches too. Shoot, he could talk as long as he liked.

"I will say this," Tony said, blowing a long trail of smoke out his nose. "That girl knew her way around a kitchen, man. Nothing like these honeys today."

"All young girls want to do is go out all the time, and the small ones can eat just as much as the big ones." Earl eyed the pickle jar Stan was holding.

Stan filled his sandwich with thick slabs of meat, carefully layering the pickles on top.

"All womens is the same." Earl made his voice go real high. "'I'm not really hungry, I just wanna taste.'" He bit down and spoke with a mouth full of food. "Women'll sit there and wolf down a whole four-course meal and have the nerve to start eyeing yo' plate."

"Damn straight," Stan agreed, wiping his bread in the juice. "When the time come to cook it's some nasty-ass meat or some fake mashed potatoes, some canned peas and cheap Gallo wine." Earl laughed so long that he choked.

"None of 'em like Flo." Tony shook his head and studied the rug. "Flo could throw down in the bed and kitchen. Black-eyed peas, collard greens, pork chops or chicken . . ."

". . . rum cake, peach cobbler or sweet potato pie," Earl said.

"Coconut pralines and pone," Stan added. They both knew the story by heart.

"You know it was one of them cakes she threw at me when I pushed her."

"Yellow cake with thick chocolate frosting," Earl said without looking up. He was licking the mustard off both of his hands. Tony told this story whenever he got drunk. Must have heard it nine hundred times.

"I came home late after that six-hour streak. You remember, Earl. I tore the place up. Nobody could touch me that night!"

"You were a firecracker, all right." Earl poured them all another round.

"Won thirty-six hundred in two fuckin' hours. Bought the whole room a round, everybody had doubles, even that three-piece-suit nigga who lost." Tony scratched his wide belly and looked at the ceiling. "Man, I was so happy. Been trying to bust that punk ass all week. You was there, Stan. You know I was rollin'."

"You couldn't hit nothing but sevens."

"I come home yelling, 'Flo, look-a here, come here, gal. Look what yo' daddy done brung you.'"

"That's when you kissed her and fell flat on

yo' ass." Stan was trying real hard not to bust out and laugh. He bit down deep into his sandwich.

Tony drank two shots and shook his head back and forth.

"She hauls off and calls you an ol' sloppy drunk, didn't she?" Earl said, holding his smile underneath his hand.

"Shouldn't have said that," Tony said sadly.

"It wasn't yo' fault. She shouldn't have called you that, man. Women need to learn how to give men respect." Earl gulped his drink and belched loudly.

"Next thing I know, she started packing her clothes." Tony almost cried, then wiped his face with a napkin.

"Um, um, um," Earl said, barely listening to Tony. He was holding a knife and a new slice of bread. He spread some more mustard on it slowly.

"So she walks out the room, huh? Earl, it's your move, man." Stan wanted him to play. He nudged Earl's elbow. Earl took his turn while Stan poured more liquor into Tony's empty glass, then he poured more into Earl's and his own.

"Man, I stormed toward her. I was so mad I wanted to rip off her clothes. I say, 'Woman, you better talk to me, girl!' I grabbed her head and pushed it against the kitchen wall. 'Don't you ever walk away from me, bitch.'"

"Called her a bitch, did ya?" Earl said it like it

was the first time he'd heard it. He sucked on each finger and then moved his checker. "Boy, I bet she was mad."

"'Talk to me,' I screamed, but she stands there all quiet, just blinking her big eyes. 'Talk to me dadgummit,'" Tony screamed again. He leaped from his seat and knocked over his glass. "She ran but I grabbed her and slammed her against the cabinets. All them damn glasses rattled like mad."

Earl and Stan didn't look up anymore. Stan took a napkin and wiped up Tony's drink. There were only a few checkers left.

Tony was standing and twisting his napkin.

"'Always quiet,' I yelled, 'ass always out of whack. Speak up, I know you got something to say.'"

But Flo hadn't said nothing. She had looked at Tony with this sad, heartbreaking stare, like a hound you done whipped on too long.

"Your move," Earl said quietly to Stan.

"So I grabs her neck. I try to make her talk," Tony said, twisting the napkin inside both fists.

"She says 'Stop, Tony. Stop, I can't breathe.' "

"I bet she was breathing all that liquor on your breath," Earl said, mocking.

"Sucking a mint woulda helped," Stan added, smiling.

Tony's face was scowled up, like he smelled something burning.

"Nigga, we both know how you can go off."

Earl and Stan both laughed in Tony's pained face.

"Veins be all bulging out the side of his skull." Stan grinned.

"Nigga looked just like Godzilla," Earl said.

Tony swayed on his feet, both fists twisting his napkin.

"So I let go, but not without ripping her robe. I tore the thing off her. Ripped the whole thing to shreds." Tony violently tore the napkin to bits. Greasy shreds fell to the floor. He slumped to his chair and downed his whole glass. "I should have treated her like royalty," Tony said.

"Queen me." Earl nudged Stan's hand.

Stan crowned the queen and put two fingers in the jar. He plopped a sliced pickle onto his tongue.

"Never bothered getting dressed. Flo just stood there, knifing the icing on slow. Oh, she had it so nice. I couldn't wait for it to be done. Nothing like having something warm from the oven, and Flo's yellow cakes with their thick chocolate frosting were the best I tasted in life."

Earl put the checkers inside the can. Stan folded the worn board in half.

"We always made good love after a blowout. The girl was real good at that too."

"Never saw that cake coming," Earl said, shaking his head.

"No, I never did," Tony answered back. "She

must have thrown it straight from the kitchen. The glass pan hit the wall and crashed down my back. Cake bits splattered all over my shoulders; chocolate was all on the wall.

"She grabbed a big bottle of whiskey and busted it against the sink. 'You put your hands on me for the last time, god damn it!' She held up the neck like it was a mallet."

"Got her voice then, didn't she," Stan said, getting his jacket.

"Oh, Flo got her voice—got her coat and her car keys too. Good thing, 'cause I probably would have killed her that night, the way I felt after that cake hit. She moved the next day. Cleared everything out. Next thing I knew, she had Charles." Tony slumped his large body down to his chair. Just saying Charles's name made Tony sick.

"I'm going over there now!" Tony leaped to his feet and grabbed a gun from a drawer. "That fool better give me my money!"

Earl and Stan both held Tony back down.

"Don't be no chump. Right now he don't know nothin'," Earl said.

"Keep playin' him, man," Stan added mildly. "Keep giving him chips, make him feel like he owes you. Percy'll do the dirty work for you."

Tony struggled free, but he tossed the gun back in the drawer. His face was pure rage but he never said a word. He'd pretended this long to be Charles's friend. But he hated him, hated that cocky half-smile, hated that young, confident strut. He hated that Charles had Flo.

All Tony wanted was to get Flo to come back. He'd love to snatch Flo behind Charles's back.

Tony got up and spit in the sink.

4

Charles and Trudy

On Tuesday morning, Charles got dressed and left the house early. He and Flo lived downstairs in a backyard apartment. It sat on a very deep lot. When Charles backed down the driveway and got to the street, he saw Percy's powder-blue Regal circle the block. Charles parked by the pay phone way down the street and told his boss he'd be out sick today. He sat and watched Flo get in the new car and drive off. He tailed her all the way to the freeway. He made sure she got on the 10 heading west before finally doubling back to the house. When he came back he saw Percy had parked. Percy was inside his car, holding a mug to his lips. Some dumb fool must owe Tony some money. Tony hired Percy to beat down the deadbeats. Charles was glad Tony cut him some slack. He rushed in and changed both the pillows and sheets and made a tall pitcher of sweet lemonade. He pressed two fat, ripe strawberries into each glass and left them to chill in the freezer.

When Charles peeked from the window again, he noticed that Percy was gone. Charles scanned the small living room once again. It was filled with old crap Flo dragged back from thrift shops. There were wobbly tables and odd chairs that didn't match. Horribly ruined bureaus with doilies on top. It looked like it belonged to an eighty-year-old maid. Charles liked chrome, black lacquer and glass but he was too cheap to ever go buy any of these things. That would mean he'd have to give up some cash. He'd never cared or noticed how the living room looked before, but he'd never had another woman in his house.

Charles socked the smashed pillows, thinking of Flo getting that car. No, he'd never brought a woman to his home before, but things had dramatically changed.

Every time a car passed, Charles immediately looked up. He couldn't believe Trudy was on her way over. But having her here was taking a chance. Someone might see her. A neighbor might tell.

Trudy rang the bell at ten-thirty sharp. She wore a snug aqua dress with a blond slender fringe that licked her thick calves as she strolled. It was an eye-candy dress. She wore it to get Charles's attention. She wanted to get in and explain the whole plan. She had no intention of having any sex.

But Charles had different ideas on his mind. He grinned and took a swig from his lemonade glass. His was swimming in gin.

"You got something for me to drink, honey?" Trudy wickedly smiled. She crossed her big legs, hiking her dress five inches farther up her thigh. She looked around the apartment. It smelled clean and looked homey. Trudy felt bad being inside Flo's place.

Charles offered her a chilled glass.

"You're wearing that dress, girl. Can I come sit next to you?"

Trudy hated that he asked. Begging her for permission. She'd have respected him more if he grabbed her right there and threw her down on the orange shag. But as soon as Charles sat, Trudy stood up. She walked across the floor to the mantel. There were three beautifully framed photos of a couple in different poses. All were of Charles and Flo. One at the beach. One in front of a church, another at a large backyard party. Charles saw them too and wished he'd taken them down. Trudy frowned when she saw them. Charles and Flo looked so happy. She began to feel sick to her stomach.

Charles saw her mood change and turned the stereo on. But the blues Etta sang only made her feel worse. It was the same way she felt right after she stole. Dumping the sad, wrinkled bags on her bed. All that stuff didn't mean nothing. It was just junk piling up. Much of it sat with the tags still intact. In fact, having it only reminded her of who she really was. Someone who takes things. Someone who lives in the cracks. No new outfit could ever shake off that bad feeling. When she stole, all she wanted was to get her foot out the door. Feeling that wonderful first lung-filling breath of escape. Having made it out the door and turning the corner, that was the real true thrill. But she hated living life looking over her shoulder. Wondering when and if she was going to get caught. Trudy looked down at her manicured nails. But how do you control your own reckless hand? How do you trust your fingers when they've failed you before? Trudy was twenty and had stolen for almost ten years. If only someone had stopped her, way back when she was young. If only someone had come up and snatched back her wrist, maybe her life would be different. All she wanted was to do this last final haul so she could stop stealing for good and finally start fresh.

Charles guided Trudy back to the couch. When he put his arm on her shoulder Trudy knocked it back down. When Charles pecked her cheek, Trudy wiped off his kiss. When he reached for her leg she leaned farther away.

Charles was nervous but his roaming hands wouldn't stop trying. Every car going by made him want to leap. The fear of getting caught knotted his stomach, but the excitement made him squirm in his seat. Besides, since Flo went out and bought the new car, Charles felt like she owed him. He was just getting his share. It was time for him to get paid.

"Baby . . ." Trudy said, facing him, placing one hand around his neck. Her thumb stroked the bone in his collar. She hated to touch him. Her fingertips ached. She didn't want Charles. She wanted his help. She glanced at the pictures on the mantel again. All Trudy felt now was scummy. This was Flo's home. She was here in her house. Trudy's eyes fell to the floor. Here she was sneaking around the back like her mother. Everything about it felt wrong.

"What's wrong with you, girl?" Charles laughed nervously. He wanted to get her inside the bed. He hoped she wasn't having second thoughts.

But Charles was sitting there scared stiff himself. Each screeching car made his arm hairs curl up. Each little sound made his head turn around. He was waiting for Trudy to make the first move. If she wanted him, he wished she would hurry.

Trudy had to act fast. There was so little time. She hiked her dress farther up the meat of her thigh. She couldn't be squeamish. She had to speak up. She could see he was waiting for something. He was teetering between satisfying a hot, aching need and wondering if he should get up and run.

Charles tried to act cool. He did not want to blow it. He didn't want this fine chick to get up and leave. So he clutched his wet drink in the palm of his hand. He let the sweet taste of gin wet the back of his teeth and roll all the way down his throat.

Charles leaned closer. She didn't resist. But when a car honked its horn they both sat there frozen. They waited until the car sped away.

Trudy let his mouth kiss her, but it was nervous and stiff. She tried to relax while his hand tugged her dress. She felt totally detached as he unhooked her bra. It didn't feel like she was really there at all. It was like she was at the show, in the dark, watching a movie. Like her body no longer belonged to her. When his hand made its way down the length of her spine Trudy cringed as she stared out the window. She felt awful. She didn't want to go any further. A lone leaf blew listlessly across the dull lawn. It rolled over itself again and again and then stopped in a harsh field of weeds.

"Baby?" Trudy said, pulling him off. This was it. This was the time. She had to ask Charles now.

"What's wrong?" Charles asked, wondering why she made him stop.

Trudy breathed deep and exhaled slow.

"What? What is it?" Charles pulled her face toward his. He was anxious to get back to business.

Suddenly the doorbell chimed through the still-silent room. Trudy pulled her dress on and Charles peeked from the drapes. He saw his neighbor on the porch.

"Damn it," he said under his breath before going to the door. "Yeah?" Charles yelled without opening the door up.

"We're leaving," the neighbor said, looking out toward the street. "We were wondering if we could borrow five dollars." The man wouldn't look at Charles. He looked ashamed to be asking. Charles dug inside his pocket. He counted his money. He held it close to his body so the man couldn't see. He had six twenties, three tens and nine folded ones. He cracked the door open and gave the man a dollar. "That's all I got on me," Charles lied to the man. "I'm kind of busy right now." The man had caught a glimpse of the money Charles had. He also had seen Trudy slip in the front door and knew Charles lived there with Flo. So the man stood there. He adjusted his feet. He looked back at Charles with a slight knowing smile. He put his hands in both pockets and waited. Charles put a ten inside the man's hand and angrily shut the front door.

Trudy stared outside at the savage backyard. A chain-link fence separated the backyard from the garage. The garage was a very old, large, run-down shack. The roof was caved in. Assorted car parts and what looked like a million dented paint cans were in there. All kinds of cans, all stacked together, old gummy colors running down the front, pooling around the bases of the cans.

The people upstairs were making a whole lot of racket. Their apartment exploded with loud, crashing bottles and the rough, angry sound of people told to move out. Charles hated living there. He craved his own place. It stabbed him when Flo went and spent all their savings. How could he ever get away from this now?

"Charles." Trudy smiled and stroked Charles's hairy chest. She didn't want to touch him, but she forced herself on. She wanted him interested enough to want to do the job. "I got a plan to make us both plenty."

Charles was listening but his mind was focused on something else. He pulled Trudy close. He circled his arms around her waist, letting his hands roam across that magnificent ass.

"I'd help any woman who had all this." Charles let his hands roam across her silk panties. "How much money are we talking about?"

"It's one-hundred-thousand dollars in cash. That's fifty thou' each. I'm willing to go fifty-fifty."

"One hundred grand. Who's got that kind of money?"

"This man I see up at the bank."

"I ain't down for hitting no bank."

"We ain't robbing it, Charles. Your part is easy."

"So why'd you pick me? What can I do?"

"Nothing you don't already do every day. Just deliver the mail at the bank where I work."

"But I'm Dockweiler, baby. That's not my route. That's Beverly Hills you're talking about."

"Look, don't worry. I got this worked out. Our regular mailman doesn't come until one o'clock. We'll be done way before homeboy gets there."

"That's all?"

"That's it. I got it all timed. All you got to do is make sure you're early." Trudy looked down, studying her hands. "But really it's not just the money I want."

"Oh, really," Charles said, pulling her chin toward him again. Charles said this last part slightly mocking her. He liked watching them big titties shake while she talked. He pulled her on top of him again.

"When Lil Steve snapped that picture, he changed my whole life." Three real tears rolled down Trudy's face. "I want Lil Steve. It's his ass I want." She struggled to pull herself together.

"Look, baby, don't cry. I'll help you out." Charles felt so good to be needed as a man. Flo didn't need him. She got her own stuff. Didn't ask him to take her to work anymore. He missed those long rides on the 405 Freeway. He'd roll along the coast chasing black-lava waves. The radio blaring. A cinnamon roll and black coffee, licking the sweet off his hand as he drove. One time he pulled off at an OPEN HOUSE sign on his way back from taking Flo to work. He didn't get out. Didn't want to talk to nobody. But he sat there admiring the house from his car. It wasn't the best house but it was cared for and clean. Straight fence, good paint and trimmed grass. That's what Flo took. The down-payment money. He glanced at the dishes stacked up in the sink. Flo got what she wanted. She didn't need him. Charles opened his thighs and grabbed Trudy's body, driving her down to the couch. Trudy struggled against Charles, but he had her pinned down. His left leg was wedged between hers.

Just then, Trudy and Charles heard the front door lock click. Both of them shot up and sat completely still. They heard the door handle turn and the creak of the screen.

"Quick!" he said, handing Trudy her purse. "Get in here."

Trudy jumped inside the closet while Charles grabbed the two glasses. He looked around fast, wondering where he could hide them. He heard the front door open. He tried not to panic. He put the two glasses in the oven.

Flo walked inside the house and threw her purse down. She got sick on her drive into work this morning. She picked up the phone and dialed her office, telling them she wasn't coming in. Flo went to the stove and turned the flame on high. She opened the cabinet and took out some tea. She figured while she was home she could rummage through Charles's clothes. She was more determined than ever to catch him.

"You forget something?" Charles said, walking into the kitchen.

Flo almost screamed.

"Hey, ah, no, no, the freeway was jammed," Flo said, looking away, walking out toward the porch. "Figured I'd come home and wait." Flo actually had gotten sick and thrown up by the road before doubling back to the house.

Charles looked at her good to see if she knew something. She looked at him to see if he suspected her. The sun was out now. It warmed the whole porch. Flo looked really pretty standing out there today. He usually saw her getting ready for work, and by the time he got home she'd changed into old clothes. He felt really bad for the first time in his life. He kept his head down. He couldn't look in her eyes. He hoped she wouldn't stay long.

"What about you?" Flo asked, glancing at him. "What are you doing here?"

"Mail carrier strike," Charles casually lied. "Only the scabs worked today."

Trudy could hear Charles and Flo talking. She tried not to breathe when their voices approached her. She could see Flo through the slits in the door. She was coming toward the closet. Trudy's heart raged. She prayed Flo didn't pull on the handle.

Charles stayed up front. He didn't want to appear suspicious. He grabbed the sports page and pretended to read, but his body was as stiff as a crowbar.

Something is different, Flo thought to herself.

Charles tossed the paper. He anxiously stood up. He leaned on the living room mantel. He could see most of Flo in the gold beveled mirror. *Don't open the closet! Don't go in there!* He hoped she didn't see the changed sheets.

When the teakettle yelled, Flo and Charles both leaped. Charles hurried to the kitchen and turned off the flame.

Flo frowned when she finally walked out of the room. She didn't notice the sheets but she did notice something. It was the faint hint of flowers from a woman's perfume. She looked at Charles hard when she left.

Charles avoided Flo's question-mark eyes. But he watched while she threw the new car in reverse. It left skid marks on their long driveway.

Charles sighed deeply when he slid the closet door open. His rib cage expanded and collapsed with each breath. From Trudy's position he could see her red panties. He knelt down and pinned her right there on the floor.

"Wait a minute!" Trudy said, shoving against his dense weight.

But Charles held her arms. His body was determined. He wanted something to erase the look on Flo's face.

"Come on, girl," Charles said. "Don't make me beg." Her standing, firm breasts looked like two juicy melons. He wanted to bite them. Let his tongue graze each tip. He tried to hook off her panties with his thumb.

But Trudy twisted and turned on the shoe-laden floor. She didn't want sex. She wanted to go but Charles pushed her back down.

"Stop . . ." she said louder. "Get off me, Charles!"

But Charles was blazed from the lemonade gin. The thought of almost getting caught turned his burners on high. He wanted some of this. There was definitely no question. He was risking too much to get nothing.

"Wait . . ." Trudy squirmed. This was not what she'd planned. But Charles ignored her and pulled down his pants. Trudy felt his belt buckle digging into her leg. "No!" Trudy yelled, trying to push Charles up. Trudy's frantic eyes shifted around the dark floor. She grabbed a leather shoe from the back of the closet and slammed it with all her might across his head.

"Are you crazy?" Trudy said, ripping herself up. She got out of the closet and left the room.

She smoothed down her dress and walked into the living room again.

Charles tried to stroke her arm with his finger as she passed, but as soon as he touched her Trudy jerked it away.

I ruined it, he thought. What was he doing? He'd never pulled a stunt like that before. He looked down at the carpet, avoiding her eyes.

"Look," Trudy, said jabbing one hand on her hip, "let's get this job done. Then we can play house. Besides"—Trudy mustered a thin veiled smile—"getting done on a junk-closet floor ain't no date."

Charles kept his head down. He felt totally ashamed. He didn't know what else to say.

"Just be at the bank like I told you, okay?" Trudy handed Charles a blue vinyl bag. "And make sure you bring this in your satchel."

"What's this?" he asked, unzipping the bag's top. The bag was stuffed with newspaper stacks cut down to the same size as money. Each stack had a real bill on top. "Hide this in your satchel and bring it tomorrow. All you have to do is be there at ten and pick up the mail from my line."

Trudy walked down the steps and hurried to her car.

"Ten o'clock!" Trudy yelled from her window.

Charles watched her car race down the street. A snail worked its way under a bush.

The two glasses clanged when he took them

out of the oven. He carried them both to the sink. Trudy's strawberry was still jammed on the thin crystal edge. Charles put the whole strawberry inside his jaw and bit down. He licked the sweet tart from each of his fingers. A line of red juice ran down his chin.

5

Flo

Don't nothing make you feel your race more than putting a perm on your head.

The god-awful burning.

Those horrible sores.

That foul-smelling chemical stink.

"You so quiet, girl. You ain't yo' same peppy self," Vernita said to Flo in the mirror.

It was Wednesday. Flo had a hair appointment at two. Flo sat there while Vernita sectioned her hair. She watched while she mixed a batch of white, putrid stuff. The short, chubby tub, the small plastic spatula she used, the hospital gloves on her wrists. The room was so warm, Flo had to sip some water. The toxic fumes mixed with the dank, angry smell of hair sizzled to the root were slowly making Flo sick.

Truth was, Flo was fuming herself. As the lye

began eating the first layer of her scalp, all she could think of was Charles.

Charles was fucking up again. Now she was sure. Flo sat there remembering how bad she felt last time. How he begged the next day, how he called the girl "dog food," some co-worker whore, then he swore that he'd never stray again.

"Dump him," her grandmother had said when she called. "The dog that bites once bites again."

Flo felt that first tingle, knew there wasn't much time before the sting started working her brain. All she could think of was burning hot ovens, barbecue pits filled with piping-hot coals, cayenne that burned the first layer off your tongue, and Charles out fucking up again. She sat perfectly still while her tender scalp blazed and the searing rage blistered her heart.

There was definitely nothing fun about getting a perm, unless you were washing it out.

Flo left the shop and got back in the car. The new car had lost all appeal for her now. She felt tired, and this flu feeling would not go away. She stopped at the drugstore down the street. She bought some Theraflu and some Tylenol PM, but as the man rang her up she bolted from the line, racing to the feminine products aisle, and picked up a pregnancy test.

When she pulled in her driveway, Charles was nowhere to be found. Flo got out, clutching the brown paper sack with the pregnancy test and a rustling bag of barbecue chips. She'd bought the chips to hide the pink pregnancy-test box from those nosy folks standing in line.

She ripped the package, peeling open the instruction sheet.

"Please, Lord," she said out loud to herself, "please don't let me be pregnant this time. Don't make me go through all that madness again."

Flo squatted over the toilet seat and peed in a blue cup. She put the cup on the sink and stuck in the wand. She paced the floor for the ten endless minutes the test took, while the test rested on the sink's counter. Finally it was time to pull out the wand. But in her eagerness she accidentally knocked the plastic cup over. Flo bent to her knees to wipe up the mess. She prayed before she looked up again. But at the tip of the wand, there was definitely no mistake. A dark blue plus sign had appeared at the tip. Big and clear as the day.

Positive! Oh, God! It can't be positive again. Flo tossed the kit in the small bathroom trash. She laid some tissues on top to hide it.

It can't be positive. Please, Lord, not now! I can't be pregnant again.

Flo jumped in her car and drove halfway across town to the free clinic on the west side.

She waited. Her face was stuck inside a magazine, but Flo wasn't reading at all. She was studying the other women who sat in the clinic. Women with two or three children already. Young ones with boyfriends parked out in front. Older ones sitting there staring straight ahead. Most of them looked scared. Their faces etched in worry. Like they were all waiting for some terrible lottery that half of them were guaranteed to win.

Someone came out and called Flo's name.

A woman in a peach doctor's coat brought her to the back room. Technicians were testing the clear yellow liquid. One of them stopped and looked up.

"It's positive," the woman said. "If you'd like to make an appoint—"

Flo turned and ran quickly back to her car. Her hands gripped the steering wheel so hard, her knuckles turned pale and went numb.

It can't be positive, she thought. *Not now, not like this.*

There was a time when Charles and she had discussed having a child. It was when his hand cupped her face under the cool steel moon. When he'd whisper and tell her he wanted a daughter. A little girl who'd look just like her. He would hold Flo so tight, bring her close to his chest or nibble against her plump stomach.

But all that seemed like a long time ago. Now when Charles got in the bed, he just pulled all the covers across his muscular back and the next thing she knew he was snoring. And that last time! Well, that was so awful that Flo had silently cried herself to sleep when it was over. Her eyes welled just thinking of it now.

Flo drove with the radio off and all the windows rolled down. She couldn't stop feeling nauseous. Her stomach did flips. She felt like she was stuffed on an over-packed bus with fifteen aggressive perfumes stealing what was left of the air.

Damn, I'm pregnant, Flo thought. *I'm pregnant again.*

Even though Charles was her man, Flo felt it was over. Deep inside Flo could feel he was already gone. She drove, half-conscious, until she reached her long driveway. She parked and walked inside the house. She saw the light blinking on the message machine and pushed play.

There on the box was the high-pitched voice of a female she didn't recognize.

"Charles," the voice said low, "be there at ten." The message clicked off after that.

Whose voice was that? It sounded familiar. Flo played the message over and over again, standing in the kitchen, right next to her knives.

Finally it dawned on her whose the voice was. Trudy! So he was seeing her! That bitch had the nerve to call Charles at home? Where the hell was his trifling ass at?

Flo'd been watching Charles these last few days, before he left the house. The way he dressed, the way he smelled, the way he paid extra attention to his hair and teeth. Humming to himself while he ironed his pants. It was the way he took his time, never once looking at her. Blind to Flo standing there grinding her teeth.

It wasn't easy watching your man get ready to go see another woman. It felt like all four burners on a stove set on High. It made tears leak like lava from her red, bloodshot eyes. She felt vicious, a lot more animal inside. Like she wanted to break something or bite down really hard, or rip something up like a stray does your trash.

Flo stood in the kitchen thinking of gunshots and skid marks on the center divide, but mostly she thought of revenge.

6

Ray Ray and Lil Steve

Lil Steve woke to fingernails tapping his car. He was sleeping good from a half-hour shower at the gym he'd taken real early that morning.

"Good morning," Vernita said, peering at him through the glass.

Lil Steve squinted while rolling down his car window. The cool air killed the hairs on his arm. L.A. was a desert. It could be one hundred degrees by day and drop to forty in the wee hours of morning.

"Get in," he said. "It's too chilly to keep this open."

"No, baby, I gotta go." Vernita pointed to her car. "I just wanted to talk to you a second."

"You always gotta go. Why don't you break a brother off proper?"

Vernita smiled and slipped into the passenger's seat.

"Can you braid my hair, please? I need to look corporate." Lil Steve always snatched whatever that person was selling. Whatever they had, he wanted it for free. "And zigzag one side and tuck the ends when you finish."

Placing his back on her seat, Lil Steve leaned his head over and Vernita skillfully plaited his hair. The only reason she was there was to make sure Lil Steve was ready. This was Friday. Today was the day. Trudy told her to come early. She wanted her to make sure he didn't get high and forget.

"So what up, baby? Tell me what you need." Lil Steve smiled, rubbing his hands over his wide-open knees.

Vernita examined his neck. He smelled nice and looked clean and was as scrubbed as a Catholic-school nun. She braided his hair with speed and finesse. All she had to do was fake a quick question.

"I just wanted to know the hot picks for tonight's fight." Vernita didn't want to bet. She hated losing money. But it was the perfect reason to tap on his door.

Lil Steve loved attention. He drank that shit up. He'd give a big long speech if anyone asked him a question. Truth be told, not too many folks did.

Lil Steve scratched his head, like he was pondering the question. He studied the birds on the telephone line. Unzipping a toiletry bag, he pulled out a fine-tooth comb and a tiny black handheld mirror that was cracked. He carefully began combing down his mustache.

Vernita watched his eyes in the tiny mirror and smiled.

"Jones. Put your hair money on him." Lil Steve rubbed his goatee and pushed black glasses over his eyes. "Liston swore he'd knock Jones out in three, but I wouldn't trust Liston. Always running off at the jib. The smart money's going against him."

Vernita finished his hair. She looked into his eyes. "Okay, you're all set."

Lil Steve got up and pulled an Armani suit from the trunk. He ducked in the backseat, expertly changed his clothes and rose from the seat looking like a stockbroker.

"Damn, you look like you're going on a job interview, honey." She rarely saw him in anything but head-to-toe Nike gear. That brother had more Air Jordans than the law allowed. He polished his Gucci sunglasses and pushed a C-note inside his sock. He'd boosted two Compaq laptops that morning at the gym. The rest of his money slept under his car mat. His trunk was a stock room. It was filled with boxes, stereos, radios and speakers for your car, laptops and digital cameras. Leather coats with security tags still on, mini vacuums, thirteen-inch television sets and a whole row of new tennis shoes.

"So are you ready?" Vernita asked.

Lil Steve sidestepped this question. He knew Vernita knew about the job but he didn't know how much, and he was never one to show his hand.

"I stay ready, baby." Lil Steve smiled, pulling a gun from under the seat. "Y'all better recognize," he said as he put the gun back.

Seeing the gun immediately made Vernita nervous, and she hurriedly got out of his car.

"Wait. Can you give me a ride to my partner on 39th?"

Vernita managed a weak smile. That brother sure was something. A real pretty boy. A handsome thug with cut features. Lil Steve didn't have much, but you'd never know from how he dressed. And you sure wouldn't suspect that he lived in his car. He always looked so fresh and clean.

It was too bad she wouldn't be hanging with Lil Steve anymore. It had been fun planting seeds and pumping him up with information. Oh well, she said, gliding the key into her car door. This life was about to be her past.

"I appreciate this, baby." Lil Steve hopped into her 5.0 Mustang. "My transmission is starting to slip."

Vernita roared her big V8 engine and let the top down. The car was a dark turquoise green that sparkled in the sun, with chrome rims and a white convertible top.

Lil Steve admired Vernita's new car. "Damn, girl, you got the freshest ride in the streets. Riding down the street witcho brains all blown out."

"Brains blown?"

"That's a convertible, girl! Damn, I sho' love these five-ohs."

Vernita rolled down Crenshaw Boulevard until they hit 39th. "Goin' Back to Cali" shook her woofers and tweeters. Biggie Smalls had just been gunned down that year.

"Turn here," Lil Steve told her.

Vernita glided her Mustang into the driveway. "This it?" she asked, leaving the ignition on.

The apartment had a few dead cars on the lawn; a washing machine was left on the front porch and there were some rose bushes that looked like barbed wire.

"Baby?" Lil Steve kissed Vernita's hand. His lips pressed the fake diamonds she had drilled in each pinkie. "Can I borrow a yard 'til tonight?" He smiled and brushed his palm across her warm cheek. Lil Steve clocked a whole lot of loose cash like this. He'd been unsnapping purses all over town. Beauticians were notorious for carrying lots of money. Fixing hair has always been a cash-friendly business. He knew plenty of men who macked the hell out of beauticians just to get next to them ends.

Vernita sighed mildly and opened her wallet.

She knew Lil Steve's thing was milking honeys for money. She took out a five, holding out the crumpled bill. "Sorry, babe," she lied, "but that's all I have." Shutting her purse tight, she put the car in reverse and held the brake until Lil Steve hopped out of the car.

Lil Steve scowled but he shoved the bill into his pocket. He didn't have time to mack her down and get more. He watched her roll back her car.

"Hey, wait!" Lil Steve screamed. "Call me, all right? Don't make a brother wait so long, either. You know that shit ain't right." He smiled at himself and combed his thin mustache. He may have gotten only five bucks today but there was definitely going to be more. Watching Vernita's shaved skull leave, Lil Steve's tongue licked his lips. It was only a matter of time.

Vernita glided her car into Drive. As she started to pull away she saw Ray Ray come outside. Ray Ray had that hard penitentiary look. The sun showed the hideous burn mark on his face. He had a coffee cup in one hand and wore black low-cut socks and a pair of worn corduroy house shoes. Damn, she thought, pulling off. Ray Ray sure was a mess. How could Trudy think that hatchet face was cute?

"I don't know why she's messing with your sorry ass." Ray Ray grinned. "She's a little too high-class for you." Ray Ray took a long swig from the hot fluid he held, flashing a wide, knowing smile at Lil Steve. "Got a nice looking 'Stang under her ass, though."

"Woowee!" Lil Steve rubbed his palms together. "Fool, that's my new shit. Don't give me no trouble. Don't ask for no cash. All she wants is my black juicy dick."

"You wish, homie. A bitch like that has more than your monkey ass on her mind."

Lil Steve frowned. Truth was, he didn't know Vernita. The only thing he knew was Vernita did hair. He'd really seen her only a handful of times. It was always real early, always at his car, and she always went home right away. She just showed out the blue, parked next to his car and asked for help putting oil in her tank. They never had sex, but he didn't tell Ray Ray that. He let him think all women wanted him bad.

"Let's go, Romeo." Ray Ray walked into the house.

While following him into the bedroom, Lil Steve saw Ray Ray's mother. "Hey, Moms," he said. "What's going on?" But Ray Ray's mother never looked his way.

Lying on the bed was a gray .45, a black Smith & Wesson and a short-nosed, pearl-handled, cute .22. There was a switchblade and two boxes of bullets, some handcuffs and two cans of Mace.

"Shit, we ain't robbing the muthafuckin' bank! Why we gotta bring all this shit?"

"Protection, brotha. Just take your piece and chill." Ray Ray strapped on his underarm holster.

Lil Steve had a gun but just used it to flash. He didn't even have any bullets. He leaned down and picked up the pearl-handled one.

Ray Ray picked up the Smith & Wesson and snapped in the clip.

"Damn, man, where'd you get this shit, dude? It's sweet." Lil Steve admired the steely weapon.

"I just got it, all right?"

"It's cool, nigga, but what's up? You gonna Mace the dude and shoot his ass too?" Lil Steve laughed. "That Mace'll fly back in your own got damn face," he told Ray Ray. "You ain't never had that shit, have you, man? You'll be coughing so bad and your eyes'll be crying. You'll be begging for some Primatene mist but can't have it. Why we gotta be strapped?"

"Just in case," Ray Ray said, serious.

"In case of what?"

"In case he gets wild and starts trippin'."

"You gonna shoot him?"

"Listen, I'll shoot the fool if I have to, but I ain't in it like that, G. Besides, I got priors. I ain't tryin' to get me no strike. If the shit don't look right, it's all off, okay? I ain't getting my ass faded 'cause some raggedy shit went crazy."

"For real," Lil Steve said, fingering his gun.

"I done did my time on some whack shit already." In tenth grade, Ray Ray had gone to juvenile hall. He wasn't the trigger man but wasn't about to scream on no OGs. He did four months and kept his mouth shut. The brothers in the 'hood respected him for that too. It was one of the dudes from the set who kicked him down with the arsenal. But he wasn't about to tell Lil Steve that. Lil Steve didn't claim no gangbangin' shit. He was a hustler. Took cuts from both sides. Made money from anybody who wanted to be in the game. Not like Ray Ray. All his people were Crips. And although he didn't claim in a color-line way, in his heart he wore nothing but navy.

"You ain't gonna use that, dude. Listen, if there ain't no money, we out, right?" Lil Steve said this last part real slow. He wanted to make sure Ray Ray understood this.

"Right, right." Ray Ray nodded his head, throwing his robe off on the bed. Pulling a black T-shirt over his hard, bench-pressed body, he put on the rest of his gray pinstriped suit. He hooked a silver-chained cross around the back of his neck. He brought the cross to his lips and kissed it.

"Come on, Moses, let's go." Lil Steve buttoned his Armani.

Ray Ray mumbled a quick prayer to himself.

"You the most religious psycho I know."

They both strolled outside into the loud A.M. sun. It was a clear day for a jacking. The sky was completely clean. You could see the Hollywood sign straight from VanNess Boulevard.

Lil Steve and Ray Ray went to Winchell's doughnuts first and ordered a couple of glazed before heading down Wilshire to the bank. They parked the Lincoln and waited across the street.

Ray Ray spoke after sitting for almost an hour. "Where's he at, dog?"

"Chill out, G, we early." Lil Steve finished his last bite of doughnut and popped open a new pack of Kools. "You don't want to just drive up and do this shit, man. We got to see what the dude looks like first."

"Trudy's going to point the dude out when we get there. All we do is wait for that damn fool to show. Said he never comes in before eleven."

"You got your fake ID?" Ray Ray asked him.

"Yep."

"Okay, so you go on in and I'ma be—"

"Nigga, you don't have to tell me my business. Listen, I'ma walk in, right. I'ma ask a few bullshit questions. I'ma wait at that skinny table and pull out these checks like I'm filling the amounts on these slips. You stay out here and wait. Don't bother coming in. They see two young black niggas in a bank and may trip. We don't want anybody gettin' suspicious. I'ma take my time, right, like I got a big deposit." Lil Steve unbuttoned his coat and took outa stack of loose checks. He got out of the car and looked back inside.

The car didn't have a backseat. It wasn't that long ago that Ray Ray had gotten the car. Looked like a piece of shit in less than six weeks. Brother was as hard on cars as he was on women and shoes. A rosary hung from the Lincoln's rearview mirror. Ray Ray's mother was Catholic—they never went to church, but Ray Ray never left the house without his cross.

"Remember, wait here. I'll be back in a minute." Lil Steve checked his Rolex and dodged across the street.

Ray Ray watched Lil Steve walk through the bank's large glass doors. He fingered the cross around his neck and turned his head from the blazing sun's rays.

Lil Steve strolled through the door. He paused for a moment. It was burning outside but the bank was near freezing. He buttoned his jacket, took off his Gucci sunglasses, wiping them off and putting them back inside their case. Lil Steve boldly walked toward the tall middle counter and started removing the stack of checks from his billfold. Trudy watched him come in but kept her eyes on her hands. The bank was mildly busy, but only two tellers were open. Nine people were waiting in line.

Trudy almost smiled when she saw Lil Steve. He looked like he owned a yacht in Marina del Rey. He had the tall, well-groomed frame of a broker.

Lil Steve smiled at one of the ladies standing in line. The white lady smiled back but quickly turned away. Lil Steve began filling amounts on the bank deposit slips. He coughed and pulled out a check register book as if he were cross-referencing amounts.

Trudy watched him closely from her bank teller's window. Lil Steve watched her too but never straight on. He was watching her reflection in the glass.

Just then, a short man in a beautiful tan suit rushed in through the front door. He had a black leather clutch wrapped tightly around his wrist, and his small tasseled shoes moved quickly across the floor. He worked his way through the fat burgundy rope and stood behind the last person in line. Ten minutes went by. The line moved slowly. A man at one of the windows didn't have the right ID.

Suddenly Ray Ray burst through the bank's glass front doors. Both Trudy and Lil Steve looked up, stunned. Ray Ray looked at Trudy and then at Lil Steve. He was tired of waiting outside in the sun. It was taking so long he thought something had happened. He walked slowly around the bank, not really knowing where to stand. He bolted to the bathroom in the back.

Trudy panicked. Vernita was in the bank's bathroom too. If he saw her the whole plan would be ruined.

Lil Steve glanced at Trudy. She was busy with a customer but she did look up briefly at Lil Steve. Her nervous eyes quickly shifted toward the tan-suit man. She pulled a ballpoint pen from behind her ear.

That was the signal. Lil Steve gathered his papers. But the tan-suit man still had five people in front of him. He tapped his small, impatient feet.

Lil Steve decided to sit down at the "new accounts" couch.

An elderly Filipino woman with thick glasses and salt-and-pepper hair sat in the chair behind a large paneled desk.

"Are you here for a new account, sir?" she asked, peering over her horn-rims.

"Sir!" Lil Steve sure liked that. Nobody had ever called him "sir" before. Lil Steve adjusted the tie under his collar.

"Why, yes. I'm looking for a new bank. I'm awfully tired of the people over at First Federal. They say they'll merge, you know, and I can just imagine the lines and impersonal service I'll receive there."

Deceiving came easy to Lil Steve. Lies would just float out over his caramel-toned tongue. His mama said he was born with the gift.

He could lie on the spot without blinking an eye. Lie about anything at any given time, and could speak white in a heartbeat if need be. Learned it when his mama had him bused to school in Granada Hills to keep him away from the gangs. He got out of the gangs but not the criminal activity. The white talk just came in handy. Used to get jumped for it before he started getting smart and switching back and forth between 'hoods.

He remembered the time one of his teachers caught him gambling in the boys' bathroom. The room was full of smoke and foul-mouth yelling.

Lil Steve was oblivious to the teacher's presence in there. He was caught up in a lucky streak that had him holding a fistful of ones, and his pockets were bulging with coins.

"Fuck you, punk-ass muthafuckas. I'ma spank you and have yo' mama sucking my dick. Who tol' yo' ass to roll a double six, bitch? Y'all is some dumb lunchmeat punks."

His teacher was shocked. Steven Williamson was one of his star pupils. "Come here, young man. Where'd you learn to talk like that?"

Lil Steve looked angry but quickly changed his face. He followed the teacher out into the hall. The teacher took him to the principal's office.

"Oh, Mr. Johnson?" he said, knocking lightly

and then going in. "Could I have a moment? Go ahead, Steven, talk the way you were talking a moment ago. Listen to this, Frank. This is going to be great." He knowingly nudged the principal's arm.

Lil Steve just sat in the wooden chair, staring.

"Go on, talk the way you were talking in the john. We just want to hear it." His teacher was trying to stifle a laugh. He was fidgeting away in his seat.

"I really don't know what you mean," Lil Steve said, keeping his eyes at the ceiling.

"Come on. Do some of that 'brother-man' stuff." Mr. Lawson nudged the principal again. "Watch this, Frank. Oh, come on," he said more excitedly now. "Talk that nigger talk you were doing in the bathroom again, boy."

A rush of heat flushed over Lil Steve's face. Like someone held an iron too close to his cheek. He was glad he wasn't no punk white boy neither, so none of them dumb fools could see.

Lil Steve rushed past them both and walked out the door and down the hall. He walked through the thick wooden doors to the street and went straight to the bus stop and sat on the bench.

It was not until the afternoon breeze of the valley hit his face that he finally breathed deeply again. Lil Steve never went back to school. Oh, he left every morning at the same exact time. He got dressed, got his books and things, but he'd double back and kick it with all the hustlers and gangsters who'd stopped going to school long ago.

"Excuse me, sir," the Filipino lady said to Lil Steve. "May I please see your ID?"

"Oh, I'm sorry," Lil Steve said, reaching for his wallet and pulling out his ID and matching fake credit cards.

"Will this be a joint account?"

"Oh, no," Lil Steve shot back. "I've never had joint partners. I remember Father's friend Phillip split up his business." He looked away a moment, just for effect. "You can't drive a car with four arms."

Lil Steve set the stage and let his marks fill the rest. He watched Ray Ray out of the corner of his eye. He was standing at the thin table, by the long teller line, dangling the bank pen from its long metal chain.

Lil Steve took a leather billfold from his upper breast pocket, carefully removed the elegant Cross pen and began filling out the form the Filipino woman gave him.

Trudy kept her head down. She couldn't look at Ray Ray. She really felt bad he was there.

Ray Ray stayed at the table for a minute and looked over at Lil Steve, who was filing his nails while the woman typed his name on a blue vinyl book.

The tan-suit man was nearing the front of the line. He repeatedly tapped his small foot.

Lil Steve noticed Ray Ray and turned his back on him. He gave the new-accounts lady his full attention.

The Filipino woman slowly rolled the bank-book out of her printer.

"All right, Mr. Jones, you're all set. How much would you like to deposit today?"

Today? Damn it, Lil Steve thought. He had forgotten he needed to put money into the account. He looked down into his wallet at two crumpled fives.

"Well, how much do I need?" He saw Ray Ray raise his eyebrows at him. He wanted Lil Steve to come on.

The tan-suit man was now at Trudy's window. In a moment he would be leaving the bank and gone.

"The minimum is fifty dollars, sir."

Lil Steve fumbled around with his wallet. He tried not to panic but the time was ticking away. Trudy was already counting the huge stack of cash. He glanced at Ray Ray, who was mad-dogging him big time now, his face all scowled up and mean.

Fuck! Lil Steve thought. This was not supposed to happen. He wouldn't even be dealing with this shit if Vernita had given him some money. Lil Steve felt the wet drip down the length of his back. Ray Ray scowled at him again and Lil Steve glanced at the door. The C-note was the very last of Lil Steve's money. Reluctantly he leaned over and peeled it from his sock.

"One moment," the Filipino woman said, getting up.

Lil Steve was sweating now. *Hurry up, bitch.* If they didn't move soon it would be too late.

Ray Ray walked away from the table and stood near the wall, pretending to read the brochures in the stand.

The tan-suit man was still at the window.

Lil Steve leaned forward, anxious. Sweat was beading around his brow. "Where'd that damn bank 'ho go?" The tan-suit man was getting ready to leave.

The Filipino lady finally came back. She handed Lil Steve the small slender passbook. She reached out her hand for Lil Steve to shake.

"Thank you very much, sir. I hope you'll enjoy banking with B of A."

"I'm sure I will," Lil Steve said, feeling more confident now. "Especially if all the people working here are as beautiful and pleasant as you." He was handsome in that black Armani suit. His height and goatee made him look distinguished. He could charm women right out of their clothes.

The woman smiled, revealing a wide row of teeth surrounded in gold.

Ray Ray collected his papers and left. He walked briskly across the street and jumped into the Lincoln. Lil Steve let go of the Filipino woman's hand. Flashing everyone in his path his Cherry Coke smile, he walked casually out the front door. All they had to do now was wait for the tan-suit man to come out. Lil Steve brushed his sleeve and strolled to the car. It felt good standing there in the Beverly Hills sun. Even the parked cars sparkled like gold.

7

Charles and Vernita

Charles was waiting in a midget white mail carrier's truck. It was parked right in front of the bank. As soon as he saw Ray Ray and Lil Steve leave, he walked quickly inside. He was wearing his blue and gray postal uniform with a giant canvas sack strapped to his back. Charles wore a hat and dark tinted glasses. A fake beard covered his face. He walked straight to the back to a water cooler in the corner. No one even looked up. Charles knew that see-through feeling well. Uniforms were always equated with the help. He was the worker, the last rung of a ladder, as noteworthy as the fake ficus tree in the lobby.

Charles studied the room under his dark tinted shades. He poured a small cup of water. He tried to act cool. He took a huge gulp and crumpled the paper cup. He took deep breaths to clear his head.

The tan-suit man watched Trudy's hands. She was busy counting bundles of money. A strap was a fat roll of money in hundreds, but a bundle equaled ten straps. Trudy counted out five hundred Saran Wrapped bundles, exactly one-hundred-thousand dollars. A blue vinyl satchel rested on her desk. Trudy took short breaths through her nose as she slowly counted the money.

Don't panic. Stay calm, Trudy scolded herself. She could feel the rushing drum of her maniac heart. *Breathe deep! Take it easy. Don't panic now.* Trudy could feel the attack trying to close up her throat. She stopped and fanned herself with a bank teller slip. She wished she could go get some water.

Suddenly, Vernita whisked toward the other teller's window. She'd been hiding in the bathroom the whole time. She was wearing a light linen suit with a dangerously low-cut halter and six-inch black patent leather stilettos. The blond wig hung way down past her shoulders. It swung across her back as she walked. The contrasting dark sunglasses made her look like a star. The men in the bank began to stare.

Vernita went to the other teller's window. She held an old check in her hand.

"May I help you?" the bank teller asked Vernita when it was finally her turn.

Vernita pushed the check and her ID under the glass. "Cash this for me, please," Vernita said coolly. She took out a compact and began dabbing her lipstick. She looked whiter than a coconut pie.

The teller smiled at Vernita. She opened the cash drawer. But suddenly she stopped and held the check in her hand. "I'm sorry, but I can't take this. It's not made out to you."

"Just cash it, honey," Vernita said, avoiding the teller's eyes. She was watching the bank in the mirror of her compact. "Go on, I'm sure it'll be fine." Vernita watched the tan-suit man at Trudy's window. He was waiting for Trudy to finishing dealing his bills.

"I'm sorry, ma'am, but we can't," the teller mildly told her.

"Well, for heaven's sake. Who's in charge here?" Vernita demanded.

Trudy looked up and stopped counting the man's money.

"Now, really, I've been a customer too long at this branch to settle for this kind of crap!" Vernita put one hand on her hip. The blond wig shook with her loose, bobbing neck.

Charles stayed quiet. He crushed another water cup in his hand.

"Ma'am, we can't cash a check made out to another person." The teller talked to her low. She wanted to calm her back down.

"The hell you can't. I've been doing it for over ten years!"

The tan-suit man glanced in Vernita's direction and then motioned for Trudy to finish.

Damn it! Trudy thought. How were they going to make the switch if the tan-suit man's eyes never left Trudy's wrists? Her breathing became labored. It sounded much more staccato. She hoped the tan-suit man didn't notice.

"I'm sorry, ma'am," the teller told Vernita. "We don't honor endorsed-over checks anymore. There's nothing more I can do."

"You are sorry. Now go get the manager, please." Vernita glanced at her wrist. She wore a fake Cartier watch. "I really don't have time for this shit." Vernita rapped her acrylics against the hard marble counter. "Really, it's only nine hundred and eighty bucks!" Vernita slammed her purse so hard on the counter that a stack of brochures floated down to the floor.

Trudy finished counting the money and zipped it inside the bank's blue satchel. She was logging the money on her bank teller ledger. All she had to do was print the receipt.

The manager came over to the other teller's window. His horn-rims stared at Vernita's platinum head. He'd been playing Korean video games at his desk. He hoped this white snob didn't take long.

"We don't cash second-party checks anymore.

Please, ma'am, calm down. There's no need for drama."

"Drama?" Vernita scowled. "Shit, this isn't dramatic. Dramatic is if I decide to leap over this counter and go upside your lopsided head." Vernita popped her gum in the manager's face.

The manager motioned for security to come over.

No! Trudy thought. *This is not good!* The guard moved away from the bank's large front door and now stood right next to her window.

"What? Am I supposed to be scared?" Vernita raised her eyes over her sunglasses.

But the security guard aggressively grabbed hold of her arm.

"What are you doing, you rent-a-cop punk?" Vernita struggled wildly to tear herself free. Her platinum wig shook like a big Christmas tree you struggled to get out of the house.

The tan-suit man glanced in Vernita's direction. But he looked back too quickly for Trudy to make the switch. He was anxious. He rapidly tapped with his foot. He wanted Trudy to hurry up so he could get out.

"Let go of me, fool. Leave me alone." Vernita was losing the fight with the guard. He was moving her toward the front door.

No! Trudy thought. She needed Vernita. Trudy was so outdone she could barely breathe now. She watched the security guard yank Vernita toward the front door.

Trudy printed the receipt for the tan-suit man and zipped it up in the blue vinyl bag with the money. There was nothing left to do but slide him the bag of money. Trudy hesitated but the tan-suit man looked so annoyed she knew she couldn't wait anymore.

"Let go of me, punk, I know Johnnie Cochran. Y'all done fucked with the wrong bitch this time!"

Trudy's eyes shot to Vernita. What the hell was she doing? She was talking way too ghetto for someone passing as white. The plan was for Vernita to create a mild diversion so Trudy could make the quick switch.

But it was too late. Vernita was captured. The guard firmly ushered Vernita toward the door.

"Excuse me," the tan-suit man said to Trudy. "Really, I don't have all day." Trudy had to give him the bag with the money.

Damn it! Trudy thought. The plan was all ruined. She handed him the blue vinyl bag.

But somehow Vernita managed to escape. She ran straight toward the tan-suit man's line, colliding right into his back. Vernita and the man stumbled down toward the floor.

It was Charles's turn now. He was waiting for this moment. He'd been moving closer and closer to Trudy's teller window. "Mail ready, ma'am?" Charles asked her fast.

Trudy handed him a stack without looking

up. She'd slipped the blue bag inside the thick mail pile and handed it quickly to Charles.

Charles gave Trudy a mail stack too with an identical blue vinyl bank bag tucked inside. This bank bag was the same exact size and weight. Nobody in the bank even noticed the switch. In less than a minute Charles was back at his truck.

The manager helped the tan-suit man to his feet. The guard hustled Vernita out of the door. The tan-suit man was visibly upset. He smoothed down his suit and straightened his tie. He snatched the blue vinyl bag from Trudy's window and briskly walked out the front door.

8

Ray Ray and Lil Steve

Ray Ray and Lil Steve nervously waited across the street. They both saw the security guard walk out to the bank lot. He wore the mirrored sunglasses of a cop. Ray Ray didn't like cops or prison guards either; he kept his squinting eyes clocked on him. Suddenly a blonde in a white linen suit emerged from the bank's wide glass doors. She walked briskly down the street tilting her head toward the ground. The guard watched the blond woman too.

Then the tan-suit man came. He walked in a tight, quickened pace and hopped into his car. Ray Ray's Lincoln idled loudly; the whole inside shook. They watched the tan-suit man tool the champagne Lexus from its spot. He easily pulled his car from the bank's parking stall. In a few seconds, he'd be on Wilshire.

"That's him, homie. Let's roll."

Ray Ray slipped it in Reverse and then shifted into Drive. He floored the car when he took off.

When the tan-suit man drove out of the bank driveway, the guard nodded at his car. The tan-suit man left the lot.

"Fuckin' buster," Lil Steve said. "I hate mutha-fuckin narcs."

Ray Ray drove the speed limit behind the sparkling-clean Lexus.

They followed the tan-suit man two car lengths behind. He rolled his car mildly through the street.

"All right, man. Ease up next to his ass." Watching the tan-suit out the corner of his eye, Lil Steve said, "That's right, homie, real slow. We'll take him on a residential street."

They were heading west down Wilshire Boulevard. The Lexus made a right on Beverly. They went another mile or so and made a quick right on Cherry. It was a narrow street lined with immaculately groomed palm trees. The kind of street you see on postcards saying "Greetings from L.A."

At the stop sign, Ray Ray pulled right next to the tan-suit man's car and then sped up and blocked the Lexus's front tires.

Ray Ray had a blue bandana tied around his

nose and mouth. He took out the grey Smith & Wesson. Lil Steve stayed in the idling car.

Ray Ray leaped out. He ran to the man's door. He busted the window out with the handle of his gun and grabbed the front door open wide.

"Hand me the envelope, white boy, 'fore I blow your bitch-ass face."

The tan-suit man was shocked. It all happened so fast. He'd been playing Frank Sinatra's "Nice and Easy Does It," and now here was a gun in his jaw.

"What envelope?" he asked, his voice trembling hard. He was trying to reach the gun he had hidden under his seat.

But Ray Ray saw the tan-suit man reach for the weapon. He bashed his gun upside the man's jaw. Blood leaked down from his earlobe.

"Okay, okay! Please, dear God, don't shoot." He shakily removed the envelope from his clutch and handed it over to Ray Ray.

Lil Steve revved the engine for Ray Ray to come on.

"Shut up, and start walking down the street," Ray Ray said.

The tan-suit man got out and shakily walked away. He slowed down like he was going to turn around.

"Don't even think about looking back, bitch, or I'ma haveta grease this fuckin' curb with your muthafuckin' brain!"

Ray Ray leaped in the Lincoln and slammed the door closed. "Let's go."

"Naw, man," Lil Steve said, opening his door and leaping out. "I'm takin' the Lex, dude."

"Don't be no fool! Nigga driving a Lexus is bound to get noticed. You know Johnny Law don't allow no brothers to drive nice rides, especially in no got damn Beverly Hills!"

"Man, stop tripping. You startin' to sound like a bitch! Let's divvy up and meet at the crib in an hour."

Suddenly they both heard the loud scream of sirens. Ray Ray still held the blue envelope and his gun.

"I'm taking the Lexus. We got to split up. They'll be looking for two. Put that cash down on the fight like we said." The sirens grew louder. Lil Steve revved the car and did a 180. The car made a big skid mark loop in the street. Ray Ray watched him tool that big ride down the next street. That crazy-ass fool didn't need to take that car too. Nigga made a fuckin' mistake.

Ray Ray took off. He drove in the alleys. He wasn't about to get caught with all of this cash.

Lil Steve was flying. Racing fast down Wilshire. With one button, he had all the windows rolled down. The sunroof rays danced on his skin. He yanked off Sinatra and turned the radio knob until Tupac boomed loud from the woofers and tweeters.

He looked in the rearviews. No one was behind him. He found a half-smoked cigar and put it between his teeth, bringing the lighter up close to his face. He exhaled the smoke deeply, blowing it out the window.

"Now this is it," he said. "This is the straight-up high life. White folks sho' know how to live." Woowee, this was some cool fucking ride. He flicked the ashes out the car window just in time to see the patrol car pull up alongside him.

Lil Steve tried to look straight ahead, but the cop motioned for him to pull over.

Lil Steve froze.

He never saw the cop car coming.

"Fuck!" he said loudly pulling the ride to the right. He smashed the cigar butt back in the ashtray. Lil Steve heard a loud pounding sound inside his eardrums. His heartbeat thumped just like a bass line.

Lil Steve watched the cop car get closer and closer. Lil Steve never looked over. He opened his Kools, using his tongue to pull one out. When the lighter's pink head popped out from the dash, he slowly brought it up to his lips. He had to act cool. Had to manage his breathing as sweat began ripening in his armpits.

9

Lil Steve and the LAPD

He was sweating so badly, his shirt clung to his back like gum on the sole of a shoe. Lil Steve remembered the first time he got popped. It was Beverly Hills too. He and Flash were coming back from a party. They were riding in Flash's new cranberry Porsche. Flash always had the nicest, cleanest ride in the 'hood. He had a red 911, not one of those chump 914s; it was the baddest car Lil Steve had ever seen. They were just coming down Sunset laughing all loud when the red lights shined on their necks.

"Pull over now!" the loudspeaker barked.

The next thing they knew they were facedown on the concrete, fingers woven together behind their necks. The police kept their legs spread a whole forty-five minutes, while they called in to check out the plates. Said they had to wait because the computer was down. Them busters always said that. Kept them sprawled on the street. They never did no white boys like that.

Turned out all them cornfeds wanted was to watch some black flesh squirm. Johnny Law was liable to yank your card any ol' time he pleased.

Lil Steve remembered the cruel humiliation as the other motorists slowed down to watch. He remembered how he felt when the police finally did speak. How a policeman had yanked him up from the concrete with scorn, smashing his face hard against the wall. How their machine-gun questions kept blasting him like bullets. How their racism welled in their mouths and hit him like a big glob of spit.

"Where are you boys going?"

"Why are you in Beverly Hills, huh?"

"Let me see your ID."

"Where were you fucks born?"

"Keep your hands up," the fat cop screamed in Lil Steve's face. "I'm not done with you yet!"

"What's all this red?" the skinny one asked. "You boys banging or what?"

The fat one tapped his flashlight against Lil Steve's head. "Where are you black asses headed?" he asked. "There are no cotton fields around here, boy." They both got a real good laugh at that. The fat one's gut shook with joy.

"Just tell me," the fat one said, breathing in

Lil Steve's face, "how can some black monkey-ass niggras like you all get a bitching car like this?"

"Must be dope money," the skinny cop added.

"Why'd you stop us?" Flash impatiently asked. "The registration's good. You got my license. What else do you want me to do?"

The fat one lowered his baton and jammed the tip in Flash's throat.

"Oh, so you're one of them talking Negros. So maybe you can tell me where you got this car from, huh?"

Well, the truth was, the car was legit. Flash bought a Porsche frame from a junkyard in Compton. He knocked the dings out and dropped in a Volkswagen engine. Painted the whole thing candy apple red. Flash had his Porsche cherried-out in no time. He liked fat rims and bright lacquer paint jobs. Hand-washed it himself twice a week. He wasn't about to get pulled over for some busted-taillight crap. Flash kept that Porsche sparkling. Everything on that car worked.

"Look man, he showed his ID. Why don't you leave us alone," Lil Steve said.

The cop slammed Lil Steve with his wooden baton. Blood oozed out over his tongue.

"Did I ask you to speak?" the fat one yelled in his face. Lil Steve felt the cop's spit on his cheek.

"Busters," Lil Steve mumbled under his breath.

"Oh, tough guy!" the fat one said, both his eyes gleaming.

"Larry, we got a tough guy over here," he told his partner.

Both the officers rushed over to Lil Steve and rammed him against the brick wall. The fat one grabbed him and put him in a chokehold while the skinny one held his Taser gun next to his forehead. They slammed him again and his teeth slit his lip.

"What's-a matter, tough guy?" the fat cop said, huffing against Lil Steve's jaw. He slammed his head hard against the wall.

"Lose your tongue, huh?" He held Lil Steve until his feet dangled off of the ground. Blood flowed out of his nose.

The other cop cuffed Flash and shoved him inside the patrol car.

"Man, we didn't do nothing!" Lil Steve screamed.

"Shut up," the fat cop said. "Get in the car, nigger."

They smashed Lil Steve inside the backseat. The officers checked for warrants, stolen plates, registration, any crimes that had gone down in the area. Nothing came up on their screen. The car and both of them were totally clean, but those assholes drove them all the way downtown anyway.

"Okay, let 'em go," the fat one told his partner, who walked over and uncuffed them both. Flash's sister picked them up and drove them down to the impound.

"Man, why'd they pull us over? We didn't do shit. You wasn't even driving fast or nothing!" Lil Steve asked Flash, still very much upset.

" 'Cause they can," Flash said, staring at the mountain of cars. "Because them muthafucks can."

But all that seemed like a long time ago. Flash had been dead for over two years now. He got shot when someone tried to steal his Porsche.

Lil Steve stayed focused. He had to be cool. He didn't want to get caught or go out like Flash. He was as cool as ice lying in the tray.

Lil Steve kept his head forward. The patrol car eased right against his side. There was no place to run or to hide. Ray Ray was nowhere in sight. Lil Steve removed the pearl-handled gun from his pocket and slipped it underneath the seat. "If they bust me, that brother'll get to keep all that cash and I'll get sent up for sho'."

The siren got louder.

Lil Steve stayed glued.

He kept his face straight. He clicked off the radio. He carefully placed his wallet on the passenger seat next to him. His movements were slow, methodical and measured. He didn't want 5-0 to ask him to do anything with his hands. He didn't want to give them an excuse and say he was reaching. Everybody knew how it went down in the 'hood. There were enough brothers who got shot by a cop who claimed they were going for a gun or a weapon, when all they were doing was rolling down the window or getting their wallets from under their seat.

The heat was not going to fade his black ass.

The officer got closer; his red and blue light soared. Lil Steve watched the green flashing arrow of his blinker as it loudly beat the leather-bound seats. But something made him pull his head off to the left. He saw the cop slow down and stare at him hard, then sped up and pulled over the car in front of him.

Mexicans! It was some muthafuckin' Mexicans they were after. Lil Steve blew out a huge sigh of relief. He watched the cop pull the Chevy truck over; three men were riding in the front.

"That's right," he said to himself. "Get them, busters." He zoomed down La Cienega Boulevard and hopped on the 10 Freeway and then took the 110 heading south. He took out his cell phone and dialed Reggie.

"Hey, man, I got one. Can I bring it by? Yeah, I'm riding in it right now. Cool. I'm coming right now." He pushed down the phone and put it back inside his pocket. He exited the 110, made a quick left off Gage and rode the rest of the way on back surface roads. He took out the cigar and pushed the ashtray back in.

"Damn, these rides is sweet," he said to himself. He opened up the glove compartment to see what was inside. There were some sunglasses and a black Donna Karan cologne bottle, designed to look just like a gun. He put both of those items in his pocket. Way in the back of the glove compartment was a tiny black box. He pulled it out with one hand and lifted the lid when he got to the light. When he looked inside, Lil Steve almost rammed the car in front.

"Got damn!" he said. Inside the black box was a giant pinkie ring smothered in giant inlaid diamonds.

Lil Steve licked his finger and jammed the ring on. It was tight, but it fit.

"Oh, yeah," Lil Steve said. "Y'all can say what you want, but look at Stevie-baby now." He smiled and hung his left hand out the window so he could see the brilliant diamonds hit the sun.

"Yep, this is some real shit here."

He looked back at the box and noticed the tiny edge of a piece of plastic coming out. Below the black fabric of the jewelry box was a tiny plastic bag with about 5 grams of cocaine.

"Well, merry Christmas, baby. We done hit the Lotto this time, nigga." Lil Steve pulled up to an old metal warehouse with a raggedy metal garage door that rolled up with a chain.

Lil Steve drove the Lexus inside while his cousin quickly pulled down the garage door.

"Hey, Big Time," Reggie said, smiling broadly at the new Lexus.

"Hey, Reg. Let's go inside the office a minute." Lil Steve walked in fast, looking suspiciously at the big, burly brother wearing blue overalls and no shirt.

They walked to the metal door of Reggie's office. It was a small room with a few folding chairs and a worn desk without any drawers. The only thing on the wall was an auto-mechanic calendar. Three big-breasted women in hot pants and bras were holding up wrenches and pliers.

Reg kept the place empty. He didn't want anything lying around that might be used as evidence. Reggie could pack up and move his whole operation in a heartbeat if he had to. Had already moved three times that year alone. Word got out on a place like Reggie's. Hot cars coming in got people jabbing. The next thing you know, somebody's sniffing around the yard.

He had a few mixed-breed dogs in the back that watched the place twenty-four-seven. He called them Neckbone, Raw Meat and Kidney. They were some loud, rowdy-ass hounds that stayed on the lean side of mean.

Lil Steve walked behind Reggie and closed the door. "Listen, man, I got this out of the glove box. Whatchu think?" he said, showing him the ring.

Reggie squinted after taking a long drag on the indo joint he passed to Lil Steve, who waved it away.

"I'm straight, man, got business."

Reggie held the smoke in his lungs a long

time and then let a long trail ease through his teeth. "I'ma tell you what I think in a minute."

Reggie studied the package a long time. "Gimme the keys."

Lil Steve tossed them across the table.

"Come on," Reggie said, rising up. "Let's pop the trunk and see what that sucker got inside."

Lil Steve followed Reggie to the trunk and watched him click the lock back.

There was nothing inside but a pair of golf clubs.

"See, man, homeboy don't have shit," Lil Steve said nervously.

Reggie removed the clubs and pulled back the mat lining the trunk and hiding the spare tire. Reggie lifted the spare tire and popped out the rim.

"Look what the hell we got here," he said.

Lil Steve stepped closer and saw a large package wrapped in black plastic with duct tape holding it shut. Lil Steve was about to take it out, but Reggie held his arm. Reggie picked up the tire and rolled it to his office, and when Lil Steve followed him inside, Reggie closed and locked the door.

Reggie looked at Lil Steve. Reggie popped a pocket knife with his teeth. Inside were two plastic bags filled with coke. Lil Steve had never seen that much blow in his life.

"Listen, cuz, I don't know who dude was or

what. Don't want to know. All I know is you got somebody's serious stash. Did they see you when you snatched the ride? Was you by yourself?"

"Naw. Me and Ray Ray jacked his ass off Wilshire, man. We had rags around our faces and shit."

"Whose ride was you in?"

"Ray Ray's."

"Did y'all kill the dude?"

"Hell, naw, man! Wasn't nothing like that!"

"Probably should have." Reggie put the small knife back in his pocket.

"Man, I ain't doing no murder time, dog. I'm still clean. I ain't never going upstate. No salad-tossin' bitches touchin' this ass! All we did was jack him. Ray Ray's holding the cash. It was the easiest shit we ever did."

Reggie shook his head. "Man, you don't understand. You and Ray Ray think you big-time players and shit. Y'all ain't nothin' but some muthafuckin' punks. Y'all fuck with somebody's stash like this and you get put on the short list of a drive-by. White boy probably running down Ray Ray's plates now."

"Don't go home, man." Reggie didn't know Lil Steve lived in his car. "You can drive my black Bug if you want. Don't even touch Ray Ray, man. You got to let that shit go." Reggie took a long drag off his fat indo smoke.

"Let it go? You must be sick. I ain't leaving without getting my ends."

"Fuck the money, boy. It's nothing but chump change anyway. You in some deep shit, fool. This ain't no credit card bullshit or some repo man scam. These muthafuckas don't play. How many folks know about this bank shit?"

"Nobody, man."

"Nobody?"

"Nobody but Trudy at the bank. You know that fine-ass sister I used to mess around—"

"You mean Trudy with the booty is in on this, fool? Everybody and they mama knows who that bitch is."

"Man, she didn't do nothing. That bitch ain't in it. She just IDed the dude, homie. Told us about them deposits."

"Man, that's the first place them jugheads gon' look. They know somebody at that bank knew about them deposits. And they know she, most likely, was the one that dropped the dime. Man, they probably at that bitch's house right now. Look, don't go home. Go stay at yo' lady's for a few days."

Reggie stared at the large bags of coke. "Here, gimme your coat." Reggie wrapped the cocaine bags in Lil Steve's jacket. "Take this bullshit witchu, man. I don't need no extra mess."

Lil Steve stared at the rolled jacket. "I'll sell 'em to you, man."

"Aw, hell naw, cuz. I'ma stick with cars. I don't fool with that bullshit, cuz."

Reggie unlocked the door and they walked to

the main garage. Lil Steve had only been at Reggie's for ten minutes and two men had already stripped the Lexus down to the chase. All the parts were wrapped in huge pieces of plastic and stacked against the wall ready to be shipped to Long Beach.

Lil Steve walked between a blue BMW and a gun-metal Benz. He stopped at a '71 Bug and got in.

"Don't go home," Reggie said over the Bug's noisy engine.

Reggie took a long drag off his spliff. He watched Lil Steve slowly back out of the lot.

"Don't go home," Reggie said again.

10

Ray Ray, Charles, Trudy and Flo

Ray Ray decided not to drive home either. He went to Lil Steve's car. He waited across the street for more than two hours but homeboy never did show.

Damn, Ray Ray thought. Something must have went wrong. That fool never should have snatched that Lexus like that. He smashed out his Newport, pulled the gear from Park and glided the Lincoln down 10th.

Where could he go? Where should he hide? Ray Ray drove with the Lincoln's seat tilted so far back you only saw his neck in the car.

He suddenly thought of Charles. He was just down the street. Maybe he could go and just chill for a minute. He could get a cold beer, throw some water on his face and try to get straight before heading to the club. Ray Ray parked the car around the corner, between Edgehill and 11th, in front of a jacked California craftsman. He pulled the blue vinyl B of A bag from under the seat and stuck it inside his shirt. He dashed across quickly with his head slightly down and ran up to Charles's porch.

"Hey, Charles," he said, banging his car keys against the screen. "Hey, Charles! Man, are you home?"

Charles was home. He peeked at Ray Ray from the shade. "Fuck!" he said under his breath. "What's he doing here?"

Charles started to tiptoe away but then heard Ray Ray say, "Man, don't try and hide. I see your shadow through the shade."

Charles was barefoot and still wore his blue postal pants. His white tank was damp from the heat.

"Open up, man! Shit, I ain't got all day." Ray Ray looked toward the street hoping he wasn't seen. He banged hard against Charles's window again. The pounding shook the whole door.

Charles was just about to twist the knob when he caught a glimpse of himself in the mirror. He was still wearing the fake beard and mustache. Charles peeled it off and shoved the disguise in his pocket. A fan blew against the sheer drapes.

"Wait a minute," Charles said, rubbing his eyes, like he was sleepy. He opened the door but he was too petrified to breathe. He didn't even unlock the screen.

"You know Flo don't want no bullshit over here, man." He hoped Ray Ray would take the hint and go.

"Sorry, man, my bad, but I thought you was the man up in here," Ray Ray said with a big, flippant grin. "Come on, nigga, stop trippin'. Let me in." Ray Ray turned around and looked over his shoulder. "This is serious business, dog. I got to talk right now!"

Charles slowly unhooked the top latch and let Ray Ray inside.

"So what's the rush, man? Why you so eager?" Charles tried to sound cool. He didn't know what Ray Ray saw. And even though inside he felt like he'd been sideswiped, outside he remained extremely low-key.

"It's Lil Steve, dog." With that Ray Ray crossed the floor and peeked out the front drapes. "You seen him today?"

"Naw, dog. I just got up. I haven't seen shit. Anyway, it ain't like that fool gonna drop by my spot. You know we don't hang. That's yo' homie, man. Me and him barely speak." Lil Steve had sold Flo a vacuum cleaner once. That piece of shit had worked once, then quit.

"Man, I need a drink." Ray Ray stood at the kitchen sink and doused his face with cold water. He wiped it off with a paper towel and laid his black gun on the counter.

Charles glanced at the gun. "I drank the last beer an hour ago." Charles didn't want to offer Ray Ray nothing to make him stay. What was he doing here now? Did homeboy know something? Charles glanced at the black gun again.

"You got a shot? I know you got some of that Johnnie Walker Black in the back room. Let me get some of that, man." Ray Ray wiped the sweat from his neck with the paper towel. "Shit, it's hot as a muthafucka out there, man!"

"Hey, let me use the phone right quick."

Ray Ray picked up Charles's phone and started to dial Lil Steve's cell.

"Shit, man. You want a drink, you want the phone. You gonna want my woman next." Charles came back with a bottle and one glass.

"Naw, man. Flo got that evil eye poppin'. I don't want none of yo' shit, dog." Ray Ray got up and looked out the drapes.

Charles walked to the side window. He peeled back the shade. He put his hand in his pocket and fingered the fake beard and mustache. He watched the lady across the street water her burnt grass. Sweat raced down the side of Charles's face. He couldn't believe Ray Ray. Why the fuck was he here? Any minute Trudy would be at his door. She'd already called to say she was on her way. He had to act cool and get Ray Ray to leave.

Charles took the bottle and downed a quick shot, then walked to the kitchen holding the neck in his fist. And even though this was the last of his very good scotch he drained the rest of the bottle in the sink. Maybe Ray Ray'd leave since the liquor was gone. Charles tried to steer him away. "Man, I'm tired. I got to get me some sleep."

"Straight up?" Ray Ray said, barely listening to Charles. He had already swallowed his Jack and was twirling the wet, empty glass.

"I want to get some rest before Flo gets home, man. She's been tripping big time lately."

Ray Ray got up and peered again out the drapes. He came back and shook the last drops from the bottle. "Damn, man, is that all you got?"

"I was fixing to go get a drink at the club. Besides, I got my eye on a honey up there."

"I ain't never seen no honeys at Dee's, man," Ray Ray said, looking at Charles. "Most of 'em just want someone to keep buying 'em shots and lighting the tips of their Virginia Slims." Ray Ray went to the kitchen and picked up his gun. "None of 'em got any heart."

Charles watched him put the gun inside a holster. "Whatchu know about heart?" Charles smiled at his friend. "You as ice pick as they come."

Ray Ray didn't even look up. He noticed a pack of gum on the dining room table. He handed a piece to Charles, folded a stick inside his mouth and then put the whole Juicy Fruit pack in his slacks.

Ray Ray massaged the bulge in his stomach. He wanted to go count the money. The blue vinyl bag itched inside his shirt. "Man, let me use your bathroom a minute."

Charles looked up, nervous. You had to go through the bedroom to get to the bathroom. His canvas mail carrier's bag with the money inside was laying on top of the bed.

But it was too late. Ray Ray stood up. He went to the bathroom and bolted the door. "Let me ride to the club with you tonight, dog," Ray Ray yelled out through the crack.

"Ride with me?" Charles sat chewing his gum fast and nervous. "What's wrong with yo' shit?" He had to get Ray Ray out. Trudy would be there any minute!

Suddenly there was a sharp rap at the door.

Charles sat paralyzed. He didn't dare move. Ray Ray seized up. He zipped up his pants. He took the gun out from his holster again. He hadn't unzipped the blue envelope yet. He peeked from the bathroom door and stared through the crack. *Lord,* he said, rubbing the flat metal cross, *please don't send me back to the pen.* He cocked his black gun and peeked through the crack.

"What's wrong witchu, man? Ain't this yo'

house? Go ahead and answer the door," Ray Ray whispered loudly.

Ray Ray opened the bathroom door wider. He clicked off the light. He stood in the shadowy black.

Charles twisted the front door handle slowly and the heavy door creaked as it opened.

Flo stood there holding two bags of groceries.

Fuck! Charles said to himself. What was Flo doing here now? She was supposed to be at work. All hell would bust loose if Flo saw Trudy at their house.

"Hey, Miss Flo," Ray Ray said relieved. He walked into the room. "Whatchu know good?" Ray Ray smiled, revealing a row of rough teeth; his gun was back under his arm.

Flo silently carried the bags to the kitchen. Lazy asses, Flo thought to herself. Neither one of them would think to offer her some help. She glanced at Charles quickly and then looked away. She was struggling with the big, heavy bags.

"See what I mean, man?" Charles said in a low tone. "I don't need that attitude up in my own place." He looked toward the door and raised his voice slightly. "People think they a queen 'cause they got a new car." Charles looked over and whispered to Ray Ray. "Let that bitch carry that shit in herself."

Flo poked her head back in. "I don't see your name on nobody's lease. Let the doorknob hit ya where the good Lord split ya." She let the kitchen door swing back shut.

"Shit, man," Ray Ray said, looking at the closed door. "If I had a nice woman coming home with groceries, my ass would stay home every day."

Charles grabbed his coat and a bottle of cologne. His keys jingled in his deep pocket.

Ray Ray nervously eyed Charles. He didn't want to drive his own car. He was afraid to go out in his Lincoln again. The police might be looking for it now.

"Hey, Charles, ol' Bessie been acting up lately." Ray Ray hadn't called his Lincoln Bessie in ages. "Mind if I ride with you?"

Charles didn't comment. He went to the bedroom. Charles wasn't worried about who drove or not. He had more important things on his mind. He shook the mail bag and the blue vinyl bag landed on the pillows. He wrapped it up inside his jacket. "No problem," Charles called from the door. "I'll be out in a minute." He watched Ray Ray walk to the front door and pause. "Go 'head, man. I'll be right there." Ray Ray peeked from the window and then stepped to the porch.

Charles was nervous. His stomach felt jumpy. He was worried about carrying around all that money. He wished he could leave some of it here. Not take it all to Dee's. He picked up a green glass bottle of Brut, spraying the cologne along his throat just to stall. Where could he put some? Where could he hide it? He grabbed the fat blue envelope and his coat and walked straight out the front door. But when he got to the curb he turned around and jogged back down the long driveway.

"Wait a second, man." Charles hollered at Ray Ray. "I forgot something. I'll be right back." Charles ran all the way back into his yard. He looked around quickly to see if anyone was watching. But he didn't have to worry. The up-stairs people had moved out. Charles glanced around the yard. There was nothing but dirt. A worn-out sheet blew from the line. In the corner stood a falling-down garage. Charles pulled hard to get the old garage door open, knocking down the thick cobwebs with a stick. The old garage was stuffed with all sorts of junk. Broken-down furniture, bags of old soiled clothes and a whole lot of rat-chewed boxes. The kind of stuff people bagged up and shoved against a wall and never came back for again.

Charles eyes skimmed the dim, cobwebbed room. A wooden plank was brimming with paint cans. Using a pocket knife, Charles worked around the lid of the can and then pried off the stubborn round top. He dumped what was left in the can on the grass. Gray, gunky paint oozed over the lawn. He sprayed the inside of the can with a hose. Luckily the money was still wrapped in plastic. He jammed most of the cash inside the old gallon can. He took fifteen thousand

and put it in the envelope in his pocket, shoving the paint can behind some others in the back and ran back down the long driveway.

"What's that?" Ray Ray asked, noticing the paint on his hands. "You planning on painting a house?"

Charles didn't respond. He wiped his hands on a napkin. He pressed on the gas, racing the car down toward Dee's Parlor.

Flo walked to the front window and peeked from the drapes. She watched Ray Ray and Charles drive away from the house, but as soon as their tires cleared away from the curb, Trudy passed by slowly in front of their driveway.

"Oh, I know this 'ho don't think she can roll over when she wants." Flo grabbed the egg carton from the plastic grocery bag. She raced from the house. "He ain't over here, slut!" She sped down the steps and straight toward Trudy's car.

"Get the hell off my street 'fore I kick your cheap ass!" Flo tossed a fresh egg at Trudy's car and missed, but the other one smashed on and in her halfway rolled window.

Flo grabbed her door handle and tried to pry it open, but Trudy skidded off toward the corner.

"Oh, it's on now!" Flo said to herself. She fanned her hot face once she got in the house. So Charles and Trudy were trying to be slick. Having Ray Ray show up was obviously a decoy.

Flo kicked the grocery bag across the floor in the kitchen. She picked up a box of Wheat Thins and the phone and dialed Tony. She sure hated to call Tony but she needed his help. This shit was getting dealt with tonight.

"That you, Flo? Flo Washington calling me? Must be my day. What's up, baby? That nigga showing his color at last?"

"Tony, can I come over for a minute?"

"Hell, yeah, 'cause I'm sure not coming to your house and getting my ass shot by your postal-working husband."

"We're not married, Tony."

"Might as well be. Y'all been shackin' forever."

"I just want to come over for a second, okay?"

"If you come, it ain't for no minute and you know this." Tony laughed a wild, evil, drunken wheeze, like he'd just told the funniest joke.

Flo didn't say a thing.

"What's wrong witcha, girl? Cat got yo' tongue?"

"I'll tell you when I get there." Flo hung up and plugged in the hot rollers and quickly got into the shower. She oiled her legs and combed out her hair until it flowed big and black against her shoulders.

She didn't want Tony. Hell, naw. Flo didn't want nothing to do with his nasty ass and foul habits. But Tony had something that Flo really wanted. See, Tony had a thing for guns. Had a whole arsenal over there. Had .350 Magnums and derringers too, snub .45's you could fit in

119

your purse and old rifles you strapped on your back. You were supposed to surrender your weapons after 'Nam but Tony and his brothers had kept some. She remembered how Tony would sit in the living room for hours. He'd spread the newspaper out over their wooden coffee table and carefully oil each one. He'd check all the triggers, gut and clean out the shaft. Then he'd twirl the barrel fast, watching it spin, until it sounded like those big roulette wheels in Vegas.

Tony took real good care of his guns. Flo thought that if he had paid that kind of attention to her they might have been able to work something out. But no, Tony was from that old school of women being in the kitchen and not having opinions. No, all Flo wanted was what Tony had and the way she felt now after all that had just happened, she'd suck a golf ball out of a water hose to get it.

11

Trudy and Jimmy

Trudy rushed home and double-locked her door. Her phone was sirening loudly from the cradle. Her makeup was smeared and some of her braids were dripping with yolk.

"Hello?" she said, snatching up the receiver while rinsing her hair in the sink.

"What happened?" Charles asked fast. "Did Flo see you go by? I saw your car in my rearviews with Ray Ray."

Trudy didn't tell him what happened with Flo. "You're with Ray Ray? Does he know?" Trudy said low, even though she was alone.

"He doesn't know shit," Charles whispered back. "But I'm sweating bullets just being with blood. All I know is you wouldn't be talking to me now if Ray Ray knew we switched those damn bags."

Deep grooves grew across Trudy's forehead. It wouldn't be good if Ray Ray found out he'd been tricked. All Ray Ray had was a couple of hundreds, and newspaper cut down to size.

"What should we do now?" Trudy asked Charles. She was still a little flustered from Flo running to her car. She wanted her money so she could hurry and leave town.

"Meet me at the club. Just sit and act natural. We'll divvy it all up when you get here."

Trudy didn't like that Charles was in control, but she had to act cool, let him call the shots. He was the one with the money.

Trudy hung up and quickly tossed her things in a satchel. Everything she needed was in that tight little bag. She was leaving tonight. She wouldn't be back. Her plan was to settle with Charles, give Vernita her cut and get on the road tonight, but now she had to go to the club.

"Fuck!" Trudy said to herself. Fuck. Fuck. Fuck. Fuck. Dee's was the last place she wanted to be. Besides, it was dangerous now. She had just ripped off a drug dealer's money. She didn't want Jimmy to point his flashlight on her.

Trudy pulled a white dress from the back of her closet. She wanted to appear cleaner than water. She rummaged through what she'd already packed in the bag: two dresses, two pairs of pants, three blouses, a few T-shirts, a new pair of shoes, some Nikes and a white pair of socks. She folded the handgun in a black bandana.

The gun was the last thing she'd stolen from her mother. When Joan threw Trudy out she'd smuggled her gun. She carefully placed the gun in her purse.

She popped in a Barry White tape to calm her nerves.

Suddenly the telephone rang.

"Whatcha doing listening to that old school stuff, girl?"

It was Jimmy! *Oh shit,* Trudy thought.

"Hey," Trudy said, trying her best to sound sleepy.

"Don't try to play like you taking a nap, baby. I've been waiting across the street. I saw you pull up. Now open this door and quit playin'."

Trudy panicked. Jimmy wouldn't just come over here, would he? How long had he been waiting? Why was he here? She walked over to the front window and peeled back the blinds. Jimmy's black SUV was parked right in her driveway.

"Why are you trying to sneak up on a girl?" Trudy said while shoving her satchel under the table with one foot. "Just give me five minutes before you come to the door. I've got to get myself together."

"I'm not waiting no fucking five minutes, girl. Open this damn door up now," he commanded.

God damn! Does he know? Why is he here? Trudy hung up. Her eyes flashed over her apartment. It was a royal mess. She had stuff all over the floor, trying to figure out what to pack. She picked up the little clothes pile on the floor and shoved it on the big clothes pile and carried it to the closet. Trudy pushed all her odd shoes and purses and belts under the bed. She yanked the comforter up and fluffed the two pillows. She took the dishes in the sink and put them all in a large plastic tub. She gathered the various cups and plates from around the TV and next to her bed and then carried the whole thing to the back porch and left it out there on the steps. She took all the brochures about Las Vegas and hid them under the rug.

Act cool, girl, Trudy told herself in the mirror. The doorbell rang. Trudy's eyes darted quickly around the room again. Everything seemed okay. Then she saw it lying out on the sink. It was her stash. Six thousand eight hundred bucks lay gaping from an open envelope on the sink. She'd skimped and saved, living on one meal a day, hoarding half of each check and surviving on Dee's Parlor singing and tips.

The bell rang again, longer this time. She opened a pack of Kraft macaroni and cheese and dumped the contents in the trash. She tucked back the flap and shoved the envelope inside. "Coming," she called toward the door.

Trudy zipped her snug dress and slipped some black fuck-me pumps on. Smearing gloss over her trembling lips, she gently opened the door.

Jimmy didn't say a word. He walked briskly inside. His eyes scanned her room and traveled over her body, and his breath was like an over-run horse.

"What are you doing dropping over out the blue like this, boy?" Trudy asked, smiling widely. She tried to keep it light.

"What?" Jimmy said leaning close to her face. Jimmy didn't smile at Trudy at all. "You trying to tell me what to do?"

"Shoot, I just asked you a question." Trudy threw her thick braids across her shoulder and walked away, but Jimmy grabbed her arm and yanked her back.

Aw, shit! Trudy thought. *Brotherman knows something. My ass is busted.* Her eyes went to the bag with her gun. But all he did when he pulled her was lean down and kiss her, sucking the length of her neck. "Don't ever keep me waiting outside like that, baby." He kissed her again, squeezing and rubbing on her body. Suddenly he pulled her away and stared into her eyes. "I don't play that shit, okay?"

"Sorry, I'm just tired. I haven't been able to sleep." Though she breathed out the faintest sigh of relief, inside she shook like a leaf.

"You have any Courvoisier?" Jimmy asked, skimming her meager liquor cabinet.

All Trudy had was one swallow of Cuervo, a dab of Alizé and a bottle of Merlot for show.

Trudy went in the kitchen and opened the wine. She saw a corner of the Kraft box and shut the cabinet all the way. She kicked her satchel farther under the table.

When she came back, a fat gun lay on the coffee table. Trudy's hand trembled when she handed him the glass. But Jimmy didn't notice. He was peering into his wallet. He spread five hundred dollars on her table.

"Who's that for?"

"You, girl. I take care of my boo." He took his glass from Trudy and pressed her hand to his lips. "Get your hair done, stock your liquor cabinet—shit, I don't care, baby, but make sure you got some Courvoisier next time. That's the only kind of shit I like."

Trudy sat down on the couch next to Jimmy. She tried not to look at the gun but couldn't help it. A cold fear started to leak into her body. Her blood warmed her face and her heartbeat sped up. It was just how she felt when she stole. Suddenly she could hear Pearl's voice clear as day: "Ain't nothing ever free in this world, girl. If ever you think you got something for free it just means they ain't figured what to charge your butt yet."

Trudy tried to shake those thoughts from her mind. She took the money from the coffee table and slipped it inside a book, just in case he decided to take the bills back.

Jimmy downed his wine and pulled Trudy to his lap. He was nibbling her lobe with his teeth when he noticed the black satchel on the floor in the kitchen. He scowled and looked in her face.

"You fixin' to leave?" Jimmy asked, puzzled. He pulled Trudy's chin toward his face.

"Oh, that's my Goodwill," she lied easily. "Nothing in it but junk. Every time I buy something I give something away. I'm taking it to the second-hand store in the morning." She hoped he wouldn't look at the contents inside. She figured it was best to change the subject.

Trudy took his drink and put it down on the table. She straddled his legs and bent over his chest and fiercely kissed him on the mouth.

"You bad girl," Jimmy said, holding her waist. "You know how to treat a man good."

Trudy was quaking with fear but lifted her dress. Jimmy's wool pants tickled the fresh skin under her thighs. Laying back, Jimmy allowed her to straddle his waist. Trudy usually liked sitting on top of men like this. Right in their laps. Staring down in their faces. It gave her a thrilling feeling of sexual power. But this time was different. She felt vulnerable and open. Like realizing you left the front door unlocked, or hearing a loud noise while taking a shower. But Trudy hid her fear. She learned how to fake it. She concentrated on Jimmy instead.

He was wearing suspenders with a blue oxford shirt. It was stiff like it had just left the cleaners. The tapered cut accentuated his firm, narrow waist. His wide shoulder blades spread for days.

127

He was cut. There was definitely no doubt about that. The man was six-six and so damn big and strong, he looked like car alarms would go off when he walked by.

Trudy started unbuttoning his shirt in slow motion. With her red dagger nails she tugged on each button until the round circle inched out the slit. The blue shirt fell open. His wide chest rose up, revealing his clingy white tank. Those tank tops were all called "wife beaters" now, because every time you saw a cop show and there was a domestic brawl, the man they dragged out always had one on. Trudy yanked up the tank and started rubbing his chest. With one hand she unhooked his belt.

"What's the hurry, baby?" Jimmy asked, smiling. "Relax, take your time. I'm not going anywhere, girl." Jimmy held her waist, like she was a valuable vase. Something he didn't want to drop. He squeezed her, then unzipped the back of her dress. He unfastened her bra and pulled it out from under each arm and began circling her nipples with his tongue.

Trudy was losing her mind. Her breath beat fast as propellers. Jimmy was doing things that shot all the way up her spine. But damn it! She didn't have time for this now. She wanted to be done. To be out the door. But his tongue seared her flesh. He excited her skin. With her nerves all on edge he was hitting a deep itch. She tried to resist. Her mind struggled to fight it. But in no time she was butter sliding across a hot knife.

"You act like you're starving," Trudy said with clenched teeth.

"I am," he said, looking at her hard, then slowly closing both his eyes.

"Why?" she asked, breathing in quick staccato. "Don't you get enough to eat?" Was she crazy? This fool could snap her damn neck. She had to get him out of the apartment.

Jimmy slid a wet finger along the length of cleavage. "Not quality." His hand explored her whole figure now, feeling her hips and that legendary ass.

"Now, aren't we aggressive," she said low in his ear. She loosened the belt on his black knife-creased slacks. She unzipped them with her teeth.

"I know," he said, skillfully flipping her over. "I kind of got that in spades." He reached up and clicked off the light. "But it looks like ol' Jimmy finally met his match."

Trudy laughed but a cold fear had lodged in her tonsils. She wanted him gone. She had to do something. If she gave him some maybe he'd at least go to sleep; she could sneak out the back door. She reached for the oil she kept under the couch next to a basket of condoms. Trudy rubbed her hands together until they were both piping hot and then massaged her warm palms across his thick, bench-pressed stomach. Jimmy moaned deep, and his breathing got heavy, the sensation made his massive legs twitch. Trudy ripped open the condom pack with her teeth, rolling it over Jimmy's skin like a new pair of stockings.

Finally, he just couldn't take any more. Jimmy held down both arms and began grinding her skin. Massaging her slow, mixing a warm ghetto roughness that made Trudy purr like a cub. This was good. But got damn, it was dangerous now. And even though his belt buckle dug into her skin, even though she tried hard to stay in control, the whole dam was broke; Trudy could not stop the flow. She began to glide right off of the planet. But her fear was what made the whole feeling exciting. Fear heightened her senses. It ignited desire. She was scared stiff but couldn't stop thrusting her hips. Her body betrayed her. It laughed in her face. His touch made her grunt, made her bite her own wrist. She felt full but still hungry. She felt thirsty yet wet. Her body had turned into one starved, sloppy sponge. She wanted to wipe something up. Though outside she tried to appear as cool as a freezer, inside she raged like a Malibu fire. His thunder, his fierceness was burning her up. He wanted her. All his ripped muscles told her that. His body said he wanted her bad. The fact that he could hurt her made her widen her legs. She knew she was crazy but her lust seized her mind. She dangled somewhere between sizzling bliss and the thought that tonight she might die. The panic grew stronger. It screamed in her veins. Her breathing was so intense the sound drummed in her brain. Did Jimmy know something? Did Jimmy suspect? She teetered on the edge of terror and desire as Jimmy's firm hands clutched the small of her back.

"Gimme that pussy!"

"It's your pussy, daddy!"

Her body kept responding. Her fear fueled her pleasure. When she moaned in his ear it was real this time. Jimmy's body rubbed her stomach in a maddening frenzy, and she met each stroke, arching her back, frantically gasping for breath. Trudy barely could stand it. She wanted him to stop, ease a bit some, but she heard her own voice beg for more. Her low moans had now turned to guttural screams. Her braids slapped against the hard wooden floor. The couch banged and shook the cold stucco wall. And just when she thought she couldn't take any more, just when she thought her pink lungs would explode, Jimmy stopped suddenly. He clicked on the light. He wiped her wild braids out of her sweaty, drenched face.

Jimmy glared down at Trudy with a menacing stare. His forehead was soaking wet.

Oh no! Trudy thought. What was he doing?

Why was he staring at her like this now? *Oh my God, he must know!* Trudy nervously glanced at his gun.

A sinister smile spread across Jimmy's mouth. His curled lips revealed a row of white, violent teeth. His fists nailed her wrists to the couch.

Trudy was frantic. She struggled under his body but his rigid arms held her wrists tight. And just when she thought he would make her confess, as his razor-blade eyes sliced across her taut body, Jimmy slowly moved inside her again.

He was teasing her! My God, that's what Jimmy was doing. Trudy had held her breath for such a long time, she felt like she might pass out. Each time he dove in, her body went crazy, winding her waist like she worked at a strip club, thrusting her big hips and wide, juicy thighs. She wanted him to come. She wanted it over. The terror was too much to bear.

"Damn, your shit's good," Jimmy said, smiling again. "I keep pulling out to just make it last."

He tried to stop again, but Trudy wouldn't let him. She could see he was teetering right near the edge. If she raised her large hips and sucked one of his nipples, she knew she could bring him back down.

"Don't do that. Wait, girl. Wait, baby. Stop." But Trudy smiled this time and sucked even harder and used those extra-strong muscles buried way deep inside that she saved for special occasions. Jimmy tried to slow down but Trudy's hips pumped fast. He blew up and slumped over her stomach.

Trudy waited a long time for his breathing to get heavy. She watched him drift softly to sleep. Trudy gently rolled from under Jimmy's overgrown body and tiptoed away on the rug. She took the five hundred dollars out from the book and added it to her stash. She picked up his pants and took them with her to the bathroom and quietly locked the door. She put on her flowered silk robe hanging from the knob and rummaged through his pants pockets. Car keys, gold case lighter and cell phone. The other pocket had a few crumpled-up fives and ones and a business card to a dentist. The back pocket held his wallet. She examined his driver's license. That was his picture all right, but the address was an apartment in Inglewood, not the house in Baldwin Hills. She looked inside the billfold. There was eighteen hundred dollars. Trudy left that money alone. She didn't want him to wake up and think she had robbed him. That's how folks ended up shot. Next to the money was a folded piece of paper. Trudy unfolded it and found a picture inside. It was a young Latin woman in a bikini. Trudy turned over the picture and read the small print on the back. "Hey, papi, here's the picture you wanted. I miss you so much. Can't wait to see you. My eye is almost healed, you big bruiser. (smile) I'll call you as soon as I get back from San Juan. Love, Conchita."

Who was this chick? Had Jimmy hit her? Trudy flushed the toilet and walked back to the room just as Jimmy rolled over and opened his eyes.

"What are you doing up?" Jimmy asked from the couch. Trudy almost jumped out of her skin. She still had his pants behind her back.

"Where'd you learn to love a brother like that?" Jimmy pulled her back down to the couch.

Trudy stayed cool and let the pants fall silently to the floor. She began to kiss the fine hairs below his navel. "What about you? Your mama didn't show you those moves," she teasingly said.

"My mama didn't teach me shit." Jimmy shot her a dirty look. "Fuck her," he said.

Trudy watched him carefully. She didn't know what to say. Her own mother was a sore subject.

"Listen. You don't know a got damn thing about me. Where I'm from. How I was raised. What I had to do to live."

Trudy pulled back. She didn't know him at all. Here she was naked, just had sex with the man and she really didn't know him from Adam. The one thing she knew was she had to get out. He was dangerous. Trudy definitely knew that. She had to find a way to get away.

"She's my mama, but Hallmark ain't talking

about her in them cards. Bitch had the nerve to call the cops on my ass. Said I pushed her in the street while driving my car. Ain't that about a bitch. I never touched her ass. She's the one who opened the door."

Trudy recoiled. "What happened to her?"

Jimmy narrowed his eyes. "Now there you go with your interrogation shit. 'What happened? What happened?' I'll tell you what happened. She dropped out and rolled and got pinned under a car." Jimmy smiled when he said that, his voice filled with pride. "Oh, she cried and carried on, put on a show for 5-0. Lied and said I was slangin' 'caine. I lost everything, all of my money, all my cars; I had all kinds of stuff. She said she wouldn't press charges if I left the state. After that, all I did was strongarm at clubs."

"You mean like a bouncer?"

"Yeah, but not like Percy or raggedy-ass Ray Ray." Jimmy looked at her like he knew something about her and Ray Ray. "Nothing like them nickel-bag fools around Dee's. All them niggas want is enough scrilla to stay high on. See, I branched out from that. Any time there was some real mess they beeped me. Used to call me 'QC.' Stood for quality control. Hired me to make sure the club always stayed tight." Jimmy suddenly sat up. "Say, what you got to feed a brother around here, baby?"

Trudy looked over her shoulder. She wasn't cooking this man nothing! She was hoping he would get up and go. She wanted him to leave so she could finally get out. She had to hurry up and meet Charles. Maybe he'd be happy with a bag of corn chips. She got up and went to the kitchen.

"So," she called out from way back in the kitchen, "ever get hurt doing that kind of work?"

"Not really," Jimmy said, rolling over, exposing half of his well-sculpted body. "This one fool tried to pull a knife on me once when I threw his ass out of this club." As she walked out of the room, Jimmy pulled down the blanket on the couch and showed Trudy an ugly jagged scar that ran down the length of his calf.

"I had him in a stronghold and he stabbed me straight in the leg. It was on after that. Nigga shouldn'ta never done that." Jimmy laughed. "He didn't come out too good, though."

"What happened to him?" Trudy said, walking back into the room.

"Snapped that muthafucka's neck, pi-ya! That's what the hell happened. Punk stay up in some halfway house now. Trying to talk shit from a wheelchair, damn buster. Dude used to drive this baby-blue Impala. Only wheels he got now are up under his butt. Could have killed him, they said. Just came that close. They taught us that shit in Desert Storm."

"You were in the military?" Trudy became more and more worried. This brother was a trained killer. He was hot-headed too. Jimmy was a clean and pressed sledgehammer walking.

"Yeah, but only for a minute until them tight blue suits tripped. Said I beat up an officer. Lied on me again. Didn't like all the cheese I made in that place. I used to lie in my cot and just count it at night. Had all them dead presidents in my bunk bed, baby. None of them dudes wanted to risk getting shot without getting their high on first. Some were even high-ranking officers. Shoot, they *had* to let me go. No black man can have that much power." Jimmy walked to the kitchen. Trudy took one step back.

"Girl, you sure know how to love a man right." He pulled Trudy's leaning-away frame and held her close. "I ain't never letting you out of my sight," Jimmy said.

"So," he said opening her cabinet, "what you got in here to eat?" He looked at the macaroni and cheese box, a large can of corn and three squat cans of sardines.

Trudy's heart raced. *My stash! Oh my God, please don't let him open the macaroni box.* Jimmy stared at her pitiful pantry for a long time. "You on a diet or something?"

Trudy hadn't bought food because she knew she was leaving. "I can make you a sandwich," she said, trying to close the cabinet.

"No, I like macaroni." He was reaching for the box when his cell phone rang loudly. He walked out of the kitchen and picked it up from the coffee table.

"That's okay, baby. Just bring me a can of sardines and a Coke."

Trudy got a Coke and peeled open the can.

"And put some ice in the glass," Jimmy yelled back.

He was putting his gold watch back on. "Yeah, Fresno, what's goin' on, man?"

"Jimmy, we got a little problem," Fresno said.

"What problem? Man, I ain't tryin' to hear 'bout no problems tonight. Tonight's the fight, man. I'm fixin' to head down to the club now."

"Man, somebody hit Wilson coming from the bank."

Jimmy stood up, walked over to the window and peered out. "Naw, I know you ain't talking about *my* shit getting robbed, dog."

"I'm trying to tell you." Fresno paused for a minute. "I'm trying to tell you it's gone."

"Wait a minute, wait a minute. Back the fuck up. What the hell do you mean gone?"

"Some busters jacked Wilson down the street from the bank. It's gone, man."

"What?"

"I'm telling you, they got him!"

"But that muthafucka was driving my Lexus, man. All of my shit was inside my ride. Where the hell is my LS400, man?"

The tan-suit man and Jimmy had the same boss. The tan-suit man made deposits. They

used him to hide the cash. But Jimmy had a totally different kind of job. He delivered large
stashes of coke for the mob.

"I told you already. Dude was crying like a
baby when he came in today. They took it all.
The money, the suitcase, the Lexus, everything.
Said somebody at the bank must have tipped
them off."

Jimmy snapped the phone shut and knocked
over Trudy's houseplant. He watched her in the
kitchen.

"Where'd you say you worked again?" Jimmy
asked, cornering her near the stove.

"I work for Tony. I sing and do office work at
Dee's three times a week." Trudy said it matter-
of-factly, but inside she was dying. She could tell
from the call Jimmy knew about the bank. She
was trying her best to act natural.

"Naw, baby," Jimmy said, looking inside his
jacket. He pulled out a small business card and
flipped it toward her face.

Trudy recognized her bank business card. She
hadn't given it to him. How in the hell did he
get it?

"You dropped this inside of my car the last
time we went out," Jimmy said, walking toward
her.

Trudy sat quietly while her stomach did flips.
She hoped Jimmy wouldn't notice her left leg
was shaking. "I *used* to work there. I quit there
last month." Trudy felt her satchel with the heel

of her foot. Jimmy'd already seen it but might check it now. She scooted it farther underneath the kitchen table.

Jimmy got right in front of Trudy's face. "No, girl, I remember. You said you had two jobs, Tony and the B of A on Wilshire." He jammed her against the wall and Trudy's eyes skimmed her knife rack. She wondered if she could reach one without him knowing. He was holding Trudy's face when his cell rang again.

It was the boss. Jimmy covered Trudy's mouth with his hand.

"Jimmy, I heard some nasty shit went down. I need that shit handled now!"

He put on his clothes and threw Trudy her dress. "Get yo' shit and let's go!" is all he said, dragging her out to his car.

12

Tony and Flo

Tony picked up the used beer cans from around the TV and threw out the stacks of racing forms. He was pissed that he got stink-eyed and hadn't cleaned the place better, but when he unhooked the latch and saw Flo in all her glory, he felt like the Fourth of July.

"Well, well, well," Tony said, sucking his thick bottom lip. "Come in and make yourself at home."

Flo walked next to Tony and let her body gently graze against his plaid polyester pants. She flashed him a radiant smile.

"Hey, Tony, baby, got anything to drink around here? You know I like that pink stuff you used to make."

Do I have anything to drink, he said smiling to himself. Baby girl was trying to be cute.

"Those were panty-droppers, girl, Tanqueray

and lemonade. Don't come in pretending like you don't remember. 'Cause I remember a time when you begged me for some. Now I might be getting a bit bald on one side, but that don't mean I'ma forget."

Flo got two glasses from the low bar in the corner, filled them and handed Tony his drink. She leaned, letting her healthy cleavage fall in his face. She knew what a weak fool he could be.

"My, my, my. I swear your steaks are still rare. And you ain't had no babies yet to knock them breasts down neither. Girl, you look good enough to eat." He swallowed that comment and downed the clear fluid, using his sleeve to wipe off the rest.

Always was a sloppy fool, Flo thought to herself. She got up and fixed them another quick round. She made his drink strong, pouring in tall Tanqueray shots. But in hers she used clear 7-Up. She lit one of his Winstons and took one deep drag. *I hope to God this don't take long,* she sighed low.

At thirty-four, Flo had known a busload of men. She'd had young ones, old ones, rich ones and fools. Most of them wanted the same fucking thing: some good sex and a nice place to eat and sleep. She smiled at Tony. She wasn't giving him shit. The only thing she was getting him was drunk.

But Tony had ideas of his own.

He was getting warm. He sprawled himself over the couch, unbuttoning his ripe polyester shirt until it fell and his gut poured over his belt like a half-harnessed whale.

I'm definitely getting me some of this tonight, Tony said to himself, rubbing his massive stomach.

Flo took the cigarette she lit and put it right in his mouth.

"I was wondering when you'd come to your senses, ol' gal. You finally see who the real man is." Tony tried to grab her arm but Flo smiled and squirmed away.

Shit, Flo thought, making his third drink. She was going to have to give this fool something to hold him off. Tony got up and rubbed her butt as she stirred her cold ice. Flo slowly buttoned the top part of his shirt and guided him back to the couch. Tony leaned over and started caressing her breasts. She let him rub them a long time while she watched the news. He tried to take her blouse off but Flo walked away, pretending to glance through his loose stacks of music.

"You got anything good?" Flo said, looking around.

Tony sat way back, sipping the rest of his gin.

So Baby wanted to take her time, he thought to himself. He watched her pick up Al Green's greatest hits and put on *Love and Happiness.*

Flo lit another cigarette and made Tony down

the last of his glass, only this time she slipped in two of those yellow pills the doctor had prescribed for her nerves.

"Come on, baby," Flo said, unzipping the front of her blouse and tossing it down to the ground. "This is my jam, honey. Let's dance!"

Just looking at big-boned Flo got Tony excited. She wore a giant lacy bra and had full-riding tits and a nice pair of black skintight pants. "Whoa, shit," he said, sucking his whole bottom lip. His dick was harder than holiday candy.

"Yeah, baby, that's right. You still got them moves." He twirled her around as they cha-chaed over the worn carpet. "You ought to come down to the club sometime, gal. Them jitter skips would have them a fit, seeing you."

Flo slipped his fourth drink into his hand and said, "Let's toast."

"To what, baby?" Tony slurred. His burning ash sadly dropped down to the shag. He felt woozy. He sank both his hands into Flo's shoulders. Like he was in the deep end and didn't remember how to swim.

"To that big thang you got pushed against my stomach." Flo tried to sound raunchy, like she was really tipsy too.

"Damn," Tony said. It throbbed so hard it hurt. He couldn't believe Flo was standing here in his living room. He grabbed up his glass, swallowing the hot fuel so fast it burned a razor-sharp path down his gullet to his bowel. He raised his glass, swaying back and forth on his feet. He felt blurry-eyed and wild with lust.

"Let's make a toast to that mail-carrying chump."

"To Charles!" Flo said fast, throwing back her own glass.

"This is a new day. I finally got my woman to come back."

He threw back his head and drained his glass with one long, messy-mouthed swallow. He wiped his face and kissed her hungrily and wet.

Flo got seriously sick to her stomach.

She didn't want to have sex. She just wanted him out. But Tony was all over her now. She had to think of something quick.

All she had to do was stall him, let the liquor and dope kick in. Flo decided she would give him a little striptease show.

"Take your clothes off," she said. Tony started fumbling with his pants.

"I'ma give you a fast erotic dance," she told his mouth. Flo began to unhook her black satin bra. She removed both her arms from the sleeves. She let the blouse graze across her firm-nippled breasts. Flo pulled the blouse taut, like she was holding a rope, then pulled it back and forth between her thick, juicy legs like her blouse was a giant black horse she was riding. Flo smiled as she approached Tony's rippling gut. She unzipped his pants and then zipped them back up.

"You're killing me!" Tony screamed, but he loved the whole show. He'd never been closer to heaven.

Flo laid him flat and tied both feet with his belt.

"Girl, you always was a stone freak." He laughed. His head was rolling against the couch now and his eyes were completely glazed.

He started moaning to himself. His tongue hung to one side. Flo walked over and slipped her big toe in his mouth. Tony sucked it like he was a baby.

Tony's body jerked suddenly forward, and he grabbed her and held her firm with both hands. His whale body pinned her down firmly to the couch. She was barely able to breathe.

"I'm getting some, girl. You done played me too long. Now, gimme that sweet meat you've been savin' up, honey. You know it's supposed to be mine."

Flo let him rub but she wouldn't let him get it. Every time he got close she'd move left or shift back to the right, so he never could get near the door. Suddenly he lunged hard, like he was diving over water, and completely passed out on the couch.

"Finally," she said, quickly gathering her things. She washed her hands and face and buttoned up her top. Tony's face was sideways on the brown-checkered pillow, and one hand hung off the couch.

Flo went straight to the bedroom, remembering the giant saxophone box. That's what she wanted. That's where Tony stashed his guns. She looked under the bed and yanked out the case. She scanned the box and let her fingers graze the cool steel inside. She felt a chill run through her bones.

This is serious, girl, she thought to herself. And then she remembered seeing Charles in the car with that bitch and the smell of a woman's perfume in their bedroom the other morning and the sound of Trudy's low-pitched voice on their phone and Charles creeping in late again.

She picked up the Smith & Wesson "Chief's Special" PD. It was the gun the police department used. It had always been Flo's favorite weapon. It was a satin stainless steel, 9mm chubby-handled gun, and it felt like a tank in her hand. It was a small personal-protection gun and the one Tony had taught her how to fire when they went to target practice together.

Yes, this would work. It fit good in her purse.

But where were the bullets? There weren't any inside the box.

She even removed the dark velvet that lined where the horn should have lay. Nothing. She looked in the kitchen drawers and closets and shoeboxes. Nothing. She was getting anxious about Tony waking up.

She quickly tiptoed back into the living room, where Tony snored loudly. He turned around and she felt her heart leap from her chest. She had to find those bullets and get out of there fast!

Tony was not cool sober, a stone fool when he drank, he had no problem putting his hands on a woman. Flo had to get out of there quick.

Where were those damn bullets? Shit!

She pulled out his drawers and fumbled, threw the shambled clothes inside. She heard Tony cough. She went back in the bedroom. She saw the small clock on the dresser clicking slowly away. It was summertime, daylight saving time too, but it was already starting to get dark.

She looked at the phone books stacked under the table. She went back in the closet and patted down his jacket pockets.

She heard Tony cough. She found a pack of cigarettes, a few matchbooks and coins. A crumpled stack of bills totaling forty-five bucks. She put the cash in her pocket and looked around.

Damn those bullets!

She went back to the bedroom again. She fumbled through the closet. When she got to an old army peacoat in the back, Flo found what she was looking for. The pockets on both sides were stuffed full of boxes, heavy and rattling with the rough sound of metal. She opened a box, shook out a few and dropped the rest in her coat pockets. Flo took the 9mm, cocked it and loaded the barrel. She pushed it back until it clicked into place.

Flo remembered holding that gun. It had been fun going to practice. Sometimes she would stand and imagine her target, aiming straight between the eyes. At the range, no one shot to cripple or wound. The only word around there was "bull's-eye."

Flo decided to take the whole box and dropped it in her purse. She scanned the room one last time to make sure she didn't forget anything.

She looked at Tony snoring on the couch. One arm hanging limp from the armrest.

Flo aimed the gun at him and said, "bam," under her breath.

She grabbed her purse, clicked the light out and left.

Flo drove like a fiend while thinking about Charles. That old feeling crept back and lodged deep in her brain. It was just how she felt before flinging that cake. That hate building up, that wanting to do something. That wild thirsty lust for revenge. Charles was probably sitting in Dee's laughing, oblivious to Flo as she drove with the cold, steely gun in her lap.

13

Joan

Trudy's mother, Joan, finished ironing Mr. Hall's pants. She brushed them again with a lint brush. She watched the crowd forming a line outside Dee's.

"Crabs in a barrel," Joan hissed under her breath. Joan preferred to do her drinking alone. She watched the activity at Dee's from her big picture window and the velvet-drape safety of home. Those were lowlifes. They were not in her class. She wouldn't be seen in that rinky-dink bar. But the reality was Joan never went anywhere at all. She was afraid she'd miss Mr. Hall's call.

Mr. Hall sat and smoked in the dark living room corner. He examined the pants carefully before putting them back on. One by one he slowly buttoned the front of his shirt. He quietly strapped on his watch.

"What time are you coming back?" Joan mildly asked him. She trained her voice to not sound desperate or controlled.

Mr. Hall crushed his cigar back down in the ashtray.

Joan had long since given up on pushing to get an answer to that question. She'd see Hall whenever he got good and ready.

Mr. Hall took his coat. He checked the contents of his wallet. He shoved it in his pocket and gently put on his hat.

"What the hell's over there that you've got to get to so bad?" Joan's sullen face made her look at least fifteen years older. "All I see is some cheap government cheese–eating roaches. How can you be seen with those crows?"

Mr. Hall almost smiled. He took out his keys. He picked up his Bible and opened the door. He left a giant bottle of scotch on the dining room table and walked out toward Dee's neon sign.

"Well, go on," she said loudly once he got out of earshot. "Go and be with those cheap, low-class wenches. All of those spooks make me sick." What really sickened Joan was the new crop of women. Young women. Young women with flawless, fresh skin. Women with hard butts and breasts and fresh, glistening hair. Women with bodies so firm they looked made out of rubber, like if you squeezed them they'd pop right back out. And the men, men her own age didn't glance her way now. They all wanted young bodies, wanted to touch those young spines. All of this rattled Joan to no end.

"Why can't these tramps stay with men their own age?" Joan yanked her drapes closed. She poured the scotch Mr. Hall had brought her. Once he left, she spent half the day waiting like this, wondering if Hall would come back.

As the crowd outside grew louder, the voices eased into her den. Curiosity made Joan pull the drapes open once more. The line outside Dee's swelled into the lot. She saw pink halter-topped women in black fishnet stockings. Their spiked heels looked like ice picks. Joan lit her smoke and exhaled slowly. *Yeah*, she thought to herself once again. Hall had his eye on one of them wenches. It was only a matter of time before one of them snagged him. Just like she'd done a long time ago.

Joan was about to close the drapes when something caught her eye. She put her whole face on the wide plate-glass frame. She saw Hall standing in line, but pushing her way through the pack was some scantily clad heifer. Her dress was half on and the men jeered as she passed. Joan followed the girl's backside, squeezing her eyes tight. It looked like Hall was following the girl too. He worked through the pack and al-

14

Ray Ray and Tony

The telephone ringing was what woke Tony up.

He heard Pearl's shrill voice on his answering machine. "Where you at, man? I can't hold these folks back. They all want to place down their bets on this fight!"

Groggily, he got dressed and rode back to the club. The parking lot was almost packed. He knew he was late but had no regrets. He sucked his bottom lip thinking of Flo. No Tony didn't regret being late at all. His baby was finally back and tonight was the fight. He was going to make a killing tonight.

When he pulled up, some folks were already inside and more were outside standing in line. They couldn't wait to throw their money on Liston or Jones. The sports betting was a big chunk of Tony's income. Most of these folks didn't most touched the girl's arm. As the girl turned, part of her breast leaked from her dress just as she passed through Dee's door. Joan's eyes rose above the girl's neck and she sucked in her breath as she stared right into Trudy's young face.

"Slut!" Joan savagely snatched the drapes shut. "A whore for a daughter, that's all I got." Joan caught a glimpse of herself in the mirror. She scrutinized the lines in her neck and her forehead. Her eyes frowned at her tight bun and dropped down to her feet. They were warped from large, engorged bunions.

She flung what was left of her drink at the mirror. She grabbed all of Mr. Hall's clothes from the closet and violently ripped them to shreds.

have cable. Shoot, cable lines didn't even come in some areas. But he had the hookup. Got all his stuff free—HBO, Showtime, all the pay-per-view he wanted, and plenty of slick nudey movies. And now with Miss Flo back in his life, all he had to do now was make money.

Pearl was rummaging through an old cigar box in the kitchen when Tony strolled into the room. Pearl dropped the box and pretended to be putting on her makeup when Tony walked up to the counter.

"I hope that extra cook in there is ready for the crowd we got tonight. And there's plenty more lining up outside."

Pearl rolled her eyes and kept painting her mascara. She wanted him to leave so she could keep looking through the box's contents.

"Can I take a bet for you this evening?" Tony said, leering over Pearl's bustline.

"Thanks, but no thanks. I keeps mines in the bank," Pearl said.

"No use letting it sit there and grow mold." Tony said it like he wasn't talking about bet money at all. He left the kitchen and lit a Winston in the hallway.

Heifer worked a man's nerves, Tony said to himself. But tonight was the big fight and Flo had come back. The cigarette glow revealed a smile inching out his mouth. Even Pearl couldn't mess with him now.

He walked into the restaurant to make sure

everything was ready. He saw Charles and Ray Ray together.

"Hey, man, I need to talk to you," Ray Ray said.

"I'm right here. What's up?" Tony said, grinning at the tight crowd.

"Not here, man," Ray Ray said, looking around.

Tony looked at Ray Ray, who was nervously moving his weight from foot to foot.

"Well, let's go into my office, then, son." There was a small line waiting outside the gate now as people eagerly waited to bet. Tony unlocked the gate and walked up the stairs to the office and pulled the drawstring over the desk. Charles and Ray Ray both followed Tony's back and took seats in the two folding chairs. Percy came up too, wearing a long black leather coat. He waited outside the small door.

"So what's up? You guys finally got some betting money this time? Must be something." Tony grinned. He flicked off his ash. " 'Cause Ray Ray looks like he might piss any minute."

"You seen Lil Steve in here yet?" Ray Ray asked.

"Naw, man, I ain't seen him. But believe you fucking me. If I ever catch that skinny nigga cheatin' in here again, his ass is gon' be barred for life." Tony looked hard at Charles, like he was talking to him too. "So y'all ready to put some money on the table instead of talking shit

156

this time?" Tony took a long drag and looked at Ray Ray. He brought one big leg over his desk.

Ray Ray started to pull out the blue vinyl bag.

"Wait a minute, Ray Ray. Let me go first," Charles blurted. He knew if Ray Ray unzipped that blue vinyl pouch he'd see he only had newspaper scraps.

"Look here, Tony. I know I been owing you. But I'm ready to settle up now." Charles pulled out an old envelope. It was stuffed full of money. Ray Ray's eyes widened but he kept his jaw tight.

Suddenly Pearl burst into the small room. "I knew I'd find you out. All I did was keep looking." Her narrowed eyes squinted at Tony like she'd caught him. She held a crumpled piece of paper in her fist. She glanced at Charles holding a big wad of money. Tony had his hand on his gun.

"Get out!" Tony said.

"But I—"

"I said get out!" Tony slammed his fist on the desk.

But Pearl smiled to herself as she walked back downstairs. She smoothed out the crumpled piece of paper in her hand. "The shit's done hit the fan now."

Tony scowled. He hadn't planned for Charles to pay him back. He wanted his debt to get way out of hand so he could have Big Percy break his back.

"Naw, man, it's okay. Go 'head and play. We'll square everything up next week."

But Charles had already counted out four thousand dollars. Tony's eyes bulged at the bag Charles was holding. The four G's only skimmed the top.

Ray Ray studied Charles and the money for a while. What was homeboy doing? Where'd he get all this cash? But Ray Ray knew better than to open his mouth. He stared at the money and stayed mute. Rubbing the burn scar with the palm of his hand, Ray Ray wanted to light his smoke but didn't dare move. He started to pull out his blue bag too, but Charles held his wrist back and stopped him.

"Wait, man," Charles said, nervously.

"Whatchu doin'?" Ray Ray said.

"Here," Charles said quickly. "This is what I owe you, too." Charles reached in and pulled out five neat stacks of hundreds. He handed the bundles to Ray Ray.

Charles leveled his eyes on Ray Ray. "Now we straight, right?"

Tony's eyes glowed big in the broom closet room. What were these two fools doing with all this dough?

Ray Ray knew Charles didn't owe him shit but he folded a grand and dug it into his sock. He took the money Charles gave him and gave it to Tony. "I'ma put the rest here on Liston." Ray Ray didn't even bother opening his bag. Where did Charles get his money? Ray Ray looked at him hard but decided it was best to stay quiet. Shoot, his bet was placed without him having to touch any of his own money. Everything should be gravy, but Ray Ray felt worried. Something was definitely wrong.

"So," Ray Ray said, "you gonna call the dude, or what?" Ray Ray stepped closer to Tony.

Tony smiled at the money and, for the first time, at Ray Ray.

"Don't have to. The man's on his way. I just hung up a few minutes ago," Tony lied. "I'll hold on to this till he gets here."

"Naw, dog. I wanna talk to him myself."

"Sorry, brotha, but we don't work it like that. If you want to place a bet it goes through me and I get mine. The man takes his twenty and you get eighty if your hit pays."

"Don't I get a receipt or nothing?" Ray Ray asked Tony.

Tony's smile broadened. "This ain't no grocery sto', Negro. Just sit tight, relax. Get something to drink; it's on me. Wait a minute." Tony opened a drawer and pulled out a bottle and removed the flask he kept in his jacket. "Here, I got something to hold you." Tony filled the flask with sticky peach brandy. "Go ahead and knock yourself out."

Two other customers waiting to place their bets came into the room and Tony motioned for Charles and Ray Ray to leave, slamming the door right in Ray Ray's worried face. Ray Ray stood there a moment before going back downstairs. He unzipped his bag and peered deep inside. On top were real bills covering each stack, but the rest was all *L.A. Times*.

"What the fuck?" Ray Ray said. He wanted to stand there and think, but Percy nudged him to go back downstairs.

Ray Ray didn't know what to do. Where the fuck was all the money? Had Lil Steve crossed him when he tossed him the bag? Had this been a scam the whole fuckin' time? Where the hell was the red nigga at? Ray Ray was mad. He rushed down the stairs. He studied Charles's back as they hustled back down. And what about Charles? What was this fool doing with cash? Last time they talked, Charles was singing the blues about owing Tony some money.

"Hey, homes?" Ray Ray stopped Charles by the arm. "Where the fuck did you get all that cheddar?" Ray Ray stood in his face. He saw the lines in Charles's eyes. Charles sputtered and started to choke.

His brain was anxiously thinking of something to say.

"Where'd you get it, huh?" Ray Ray asked him again. "What's-a-matter, cat got your tongue?"

The club felt so hot. Charles loosened his collar. The pre-fight was on. Two men were boxing. Their muscular brown bodies were glistening wet. One had a smashed, bloody face.

Ray Ray's face was so close, Charles felt his breath on his nose.

"Huh? I'm talking to you, man," Ray Ray asked him point-blank.

Charles fidgeted against the wall. One of the fighters fell down. A small Cuban guy knocked down a big pale Russian. Half the crowd in Dee's Parlor lurched up and screamed. Charles panicked. What the hell could he say? Where in the hell could he have gotten fifteen grand? But suddenly it hit. The lie floated through his teeth.

"I sold that bitch's new car."

15

Lil Steve and Vernita

A hot breeze blew a pack of Kools into the gutter off Western. Lil Steve scratched his neck and leaned against the cracked vinyl of the Bug.

"Damn, it's hot," he said, wiping his face with his sleeve.

He checked the Rolex on his wrist again. It was 7:55. Across town the Lexus had already been stripped down. The parts were shipped to Long Beach by now. He looked at the bag of cocaine. He had to hide this bag before Johnny Law saw him and pulled his card.

But Lil Steve had a jones or two of his own. He was real low-key. He didn't let it show. See, nobody knew he smoked coke. There were baby rocks he got off the street from time to time but he always went to the east side to cop. He only bought rocks off the *Cholos* in MacArthur Park or the *Eses* along Alvarado. None of the brothers knew he did blow. He smoked rocks by himself, all alone in the car. He never shared. He avoided all those crackheads around Dee's. He didn't want none of them fools to label him a "head." Once it gets known you base, you in a whole other league. People start to watch you around all their shit. He couldn't have that. He needed folks' trust. His whole game was confidence and macking. He wasn't about to fuck that up. That was out of the question. So whenever he did lines or smoked some cocaine, it was always late at night by himself.

Lil Steve looked at the trash and liquor bottles in the street. He peered down inside the bag. The last time he saw this much stuff was right before the battering ram busted Flash's door and hauled everybody down to County.

Lil Steve stuck a pen and made a small hole. He licked his finger and dunked it inside the powder, rubbing the white substance over his top gum and teeth. The low life was over. It was all gravy now. Lil Steve sucked the tip of his finger. He wasn't even worried about Ray Ray with the money. With this giant bag of coke, there was no telling how much he could make on the street.

There's got to be someplace I can do some of this. Suddenly he thought of Vernita.

He smiled to himself. Yeah, Vernita was cool. All them other skeezers he knew couldn't hold water. They'd drop a dime on him in no time.

He turned down Adams and headed toward 10th Avenue. He stopped at Johnnie Pastrami and got a couple of sandwiches. He saw the bright lights from her shop.

Vernita had one more customer in there. She was doing a short woman's hair. She hadn't gotten to the blow-drying stage, so Lil Steve just sat there and waited. He stared long and hard at the bag on the floor. A few palm trees swayed in the cool evening moon. The liquor store across Adams kept the grass littered with empties. Bent cigarette boxes licked the curb.

Lil Steve picked up the bag and brought it up to his lap. He carefully opened the case and looked out of his rearviews to see if anybody was coming. The black Bug had illegally dark tinted windows, so Lil Steve wasn't worried about anybody seeing him inside, but he didn't want any surprises. He carefully pulled back the duct tape that held the package shut. He took his car keys and used his knife to cut open the plastic bag, making an incision along the top so nothing would spill. Then Lil Steve closed the knife back in, pulled out the screwdriver tool and used the flat tip to dip inside the bag. He got a small portion of the white powder on the tip, brought it to his nose and inhaled deep. This was the first time he had him some serious powder. Everybody around there only did rocks.

He watched Vernita bring the curling iron toward the woman's scalp.

Lil Steve dipped the screwdriver in again.

He noticed the smooth movements of Vernita's hands. The way they worked and pulled the hair in strong, artful strokes.

He inhaled the powder real slow.

Vernita spun the chair around so she could do the woman's left side. Lil Steve lifted the wide-tip screwdriver back to his nose. He inhaled eight more times and saved some in the seat before folding the duct tape back over the small hole he'd made. He popped his pocketknife with his teeth and sawed along the cushion of the passenger seat. Pulling the vinyl seat back and removing some of the foam, he firmly pushed the plastic bag inside and folded the vinyl back down.

Lil Steve didn't realize how keyed up he was. He pulled the handle up and let the seat fall. He lay back so he could relax. Though his head barely rose above the window to see, he watched Vernita work in the large salon window. His heart began beating with speed.

He took a cigarette and pulled some of the tobacco from the top and put the cocaine that he'd saved in the cigarette tip. He noticed his hand started trembling a bit. His head felt like he'd sucked on a helium balloon.

He had the music up and was puffing the end of a Salem Light when the short woman finally emerged from the shop. She came right to the car parked in front of him, a beautiful burgundy Jag. Vernita sure did hair good. Had that plain woman looking Hollywood in no time. Waxy locks framed her soft, round face. Gold dolphin earrings screamed against her reddish-brown skin. The woman had a real pep in her step when she walked out of Vernita's shop door.

As soon as the woman pulled away, Lil Steve grabbed the pastrami sandwiches. He put a Raiders cap on and some wraparound sunglasses. He left his suit jacket on the seat.

"Hey, baby," he said, coming in and closing the door. "I got you something to eat."

Vernita was sweeping. She had her back to the door. She hadn't seen or heard Lil Steve come in and almost jumped when she saw his cocky smile in her door. Oh shit! What was he doing here? She planned to meet Trudy here at the shop. She didn't want them rough fools looking sideways at her. She spied the blond wig she'd worn laying in a chair and gently dropped a silk scarf on top.

"What do you want, boy? Didn't I take care of your hair? I know you ain't ready to be tightened again." Vernita tried to be glib. *Be cool,* she told herself. *Don't act nervous or he'll suspect something.*

Lil Steve pulled down the shades and clicked off the huge light that illuminated the shop.

Only the lamp with the sixty-watt burned. Vernita picked up the broom and started sweeping again.

"Is that how you greet a man who came all the way up here to bring you some food?" Lil Steve yanked the shades on the other side of the room. "Besides," he said slowly, "I been missin' you, baby. Come here and give Lil Steve a kiss." He put a lot of sugar in that last line.

"Boy, please." Vernita eyed Lil Steve. He seemed more animated than his usually cool ice-tray self. Vernita felt something was wrong.

Lil Steve walked across the room and pulled the other shades down. The shop immediately grew dim.

"Why you got all these windows open in here all the time, girl? Ain'tchu supposed to be closed?"

"I guess I am now," Vernita mumbled to herself. "How come you're so worried about how I run my business?" Vernita tried to keep the conversation light.

"I'm trying to help you, girl." Lil Steve smiled. "You never know when someone might come in and jack you." Lil Steve looked dead into her eyes.

Vernita was sweeping more feverishly now. When she accidentally knocked the silk scarf to the ground, the blond wig drifted down to the floor. Vernita's heart skipped. She stood still as the moon. Lil Steve moved close to her knee. He picked up the wig. He looked at Vernita a real long time, fingering the platinum hair in his hand.

"Why don't you put this on for me, baby?" Lil Steve held it out for her to take.

"Listen, I don't play blondie for nobody, okay? You want a blonde, go to Huntington Beach." Vernita started quickly sweeping again. She put the last bits of hair in the trash.

"What's wrong with you, huh? Why you acting so mean? You weren't like this this morning."

Lil Steve peeked out from the shade and then closed it again. He narrowed his eyes on Vernita.

"I'm not acting like shit." Vernita tried to sound casual. "You the one coming in here trippin'."

Lil Steve loved the rush the cocaine brought on. Though his nerves felt like millions of ants on his skin, inside his skull sizzled and glowed. "Come on! Put it on!" He shoved the wig toward her, but Vernita brushed his stiff hand away.

Lil Steve rushed up on her. The wig dangled from his fist. His face was all twisted with hate. He tried to put the wig over Vernita's cropped head.

"Stop it!" she said. "I don't want to wear it!" Vernita tried to pull free, but Lil Steve held her arm.

"Why not?" he screamed. "Come on. Put it on!" His voice was loud but he didn't know why. He was taking fast, rapid-fire breaths. The coke crept up on him. It was tickling his brain. He held Vernita down hard but didn't know why. He didn't realize how keyed-up he was when he pointed his gun toward her head.

"Put the fucking wig on." Lil Steve was surprised at his own actions. Why in the world was he was talking like this? He knew he should chill but he couldn't stop himself. He didn't even know he'd cocked back the gun.

Vernita looked stunned as the gun shook in his hand. She pulled the blond wig on top of her head. In her nervous haste she put the wig on backward. Long blond strands hung over her face.

"Now see," he said. "Wasn't that easy? All a brother wants is a little variety now and then. Men are visual, baby. We like seeing new shit. We want something fresh from our women." Lil Steve grinned as the gun trembled in his right hand. He eased into a beauty salon chair.

Vernita stayed quiet, clocking his movements. She inched her left hand way behind her back, reaching for the large can of hairspray.

"Girl, I been driving around all day trying to figure out what's wrong, what's been missing in my life." Lil Steve stared into Vernita's light, concerned eyes.

"I've been thinking about you and me all damn day long. As soon as you left me this morning I knew." What the fuck was he saying? He never thought of her once. But his pimp side was recklessly now in full bloom. As he lied through his teeth, his lungs strained for air. The coke had messed him up bad. He recklessly dangled the gun in his hand. He pulled Vernita's body inside the salon chair, holding her flat against his quivering chest.

Vernita let one arm hang from the chair. She was holding the hairspray in the palm of her hand.

"There now, see? You made me come all the way over here and say it. All this time you done got a nigga sprung." He pulled on her neck, bringing her mouth close to his. He pulled the chair's lever until they were both lying prone. Her small body lay completely over his. Vernita watched his gun. She felt his frantic, quaking lungs. They vibrated like a helicopter hovering close to a house.

Vernita was trapped. Lil Steve held her tight. But she still had one hand dangling from the chair. She slowly moved her finger over the spray can's small nozzle.

Lil Steve kissed her mouth. The wig's hair fell in his eyes. He snatched off the wig, throwing it over his shoulder. He held Vernita's neck. "I want you," he said, holding the gun on her cheek. She could feel the cold steel resting right against her jaw. Vernita wouldn't kiss him. She moved her mouth from his lips but she smiled and ran her fingertip over his teeth. They were as smooth as a row of strung pearls. Lil Steve seized her body, gently nibbling her pointer finger. He licked her two fingers as she played with his tongue. Her fingers inched toward the deep grooves of his back molars. With his eyes rolling up and his mouth opened wide, Vernita sprayed the can deep in his throat. A gunshot blast blew the huge mirror into shards. A large fragment busted the overhead light, and the whole room went totally black.

16

Flo

Flo's headlights pierced through the dark anxious night. She raced down the street like a three-legged dog, hell-bent on biting a truck. No, Flo could not wait to catch Charles now. This was it. It was on. She was fit to be tied. She was definitely going to get him tonight.

As Jimmy was racing Trudy over to Dee's, Flo swerved her Camaro there too.

Flo flew through the greens, floored it on yellows and when she had to stop once at the blaring red flame, she took off before it changed back. At last, there it was, Dee's Parlor's rusty orange neon, laughing at her from the gloom. Flo slowed and pulled into Dee's gravel lot. There was a green awning over the large wooden door. The club did its best to look upscale outside but this hit-and-run parking lot said it all. Potholes full of old, stagnant water. Smashed cans of beer and miniature bottles of liquor. Bloated cigarette butts floating in dank, murky puddles like hundreds of tiny drowned bodies.

Flo eased in and rolled to the back of the lot. She didn't want to be seen by the huge wad of people choking the front door.

She rammed the brake down, put the car in Park and was dabbing her lipstick when she heard the grinding sound of wheels on rock. That was one good thing about the lot next to Dee's. You could always hear when someone pulled in. Those pebbles barked loud under your tires.

Flo slithered down a few inches and watched an older couple go inside. She wanted to get out of the freak clothes she'd worn for Tony and put on the jumpsuit she had in the trunk.

Flo got out of the car and inched her leather pants off. She opened the trunk, taking a black jumpsuit from a plastic cleaner's bag, and stepped one leg inside. Just as she was about to pull her leg through the hole, she heard the loud crunching sound of gravel. Flo ducked down behind her fender to avoid the headlights. A giant black Suburban pulled in and parked two spaces from hers. The headlights illuminated the parking lot so much that Flo had to press herself flat against the fender and door. A big man waited a long time before he got out. He looked like he was arguing with the person inside. Suddenly, the man looked over her way. But Flo was no fool. She stood still, didn't move. She held her breath until the man looked away.

Flo hurried her other foot into the other pants leg and zipped the suit up to her neck. She could hear angry shouting coming from inside the car. She slowly lifted her head and peeked over her hood to take a look. But before she could see, she heard a door open and slam, so she ducked her head down again. There was a crumbling-gravel sound of large heavy feet, and Flo peeked up over the hood to see.

The big man was yelling loud. He was furiously upset. His arms were hawked up and his huge chest was swollen. He ran over, yanked open the passenger side and screamed.

"Get out!" he yelled to the person inside.

A silhouette slithered out from the seat.

When the streetlight hit the woman, Flo could see her pained face. "Well, I'll be," Flo said, recognizing her now. It was Trudy. "I guess having my man ain't enough for her trifling ass. Them chickens finally came home to roost."

But when Flo moved to adjust her foot, which had fallen asleep, she accidentally dropped her car keys.

"What was that?" Jimmy said. "Didn't you hear something?" he said to Trudy.

Pulling out his gun, Jimmy started over toward Flo's car.

Flo didn't know what to do. She was shaking in fear. The man was almost at her car! Flo slithered around her fender, ducking lower than before.

Jimmy stood next to Flo's passenger side. She could hear him breathing. She watched him peer inside. He waited a long time before he finally put his gun back and turned around. While Jimmy was gone, Trudy inched toward the club's door, but Jimmy grabbed her arm like a hostage.

"Where the fuck do you think you're going?"

Trudy hung her head and froze.

Her dress slipped from her shoulder and Flo saw her full breast. It loomed large under the orange neon moon.

Jimmy grabbed her, yanking her hard through the densely packed crowd. Trudy tried to cover her body. Her dress flopped off one side. The zipper was all the way down in the back.

"Whatchu say, Percy," Jimmy said, giving a pound without smiling.

"You got the winning hand," Percy said, gazing at Trudy's backside.

Jimmy slipped him a fifty. "Keep an eye on her, man. Don't let her out of your sight."

"I don't mind putting in work for you, homes." Percy sucked his tongue until it smacked.

Flo quickly got back inside her car. She needed to catch her breath. She needed to think. Flo decided to move her car forward and park where she could watch Dee's busy front door.

17

Trudy and Jimmy

"Stick him!"

"Throw that right again, man!"

"Don't show that sucka you weak."

The club was filled up. People were packed to the rafters. The fight blared on three television sets: a big screen, a nineteen-inch over the bar and a thirteen-inch with no color left that sat by the cook in the kitchen. Even people who normally didn't go to Dee's Parlor were sitting there slinging back beer after beer, laughing and munching on chips.

The ring girl grinned big. She was all lips and thighs. No one could see the large wart on her hand.

Ed "Meatloaf" Jones and Billy "The Hitman" Liston stood glistening on the taut canvas floor.

Glaring, they looked anxious to finish the assault. The referee stood in between.

Ray Ray's eyes were glued to Dee's Parlor's front door. He hadn't seen Trudy yet or Lil Steve either. He got up and skimmed the packed parking lot, then he walked all the way back to the kitchen.

At that moment, Charles saw Jimmy pull Trudy in. Aw shit, he thought! Trudy got popped. What could he do? He better sit and stay quiet. But when Jimmy ran upstairs, leaving Trudy alone, Charles pushed his way to her table.

"Is this seat taken?" Charles looked at Percy.

"Yeah," Percy said, mad-dogging him hard. Trudy flipped her braids and rolled her eyes up at Percy.

Charles stood by the table but didn't sit down.

"You all right?" Charles asked, talking low.

Trudy gave a quick shake "no." Charles stared in her eyes; they were red like she had been crying.

Jimmy was coming back downstairs again. He was rapidly talking to two well-dressed men. One of them started to shout. When Jimmy saw Charles standing next to Trudy, he stormed over to the table, knocking over a glass.

"Who the fuck are you?" Jimmy angrily screamed.

Charles looked down. He wished Ray Ray were there.

"I asked you a question. You mute, mutha-fucka?" Jimmy stepped up to his face.

Charles stuck out his hand. "Charles," he said fast. Charles didn't have a clue who Jimmy was, but he looked like a man you don't mess with.

Jimmy stared at Charles's hand but just left it hanging.

Charles put his hand in his pocket.

Jimmy abruptly snatched Trudy up from her seat.

Charles wanted to say something but he scanned Jimmy's wide body. It had already bumped the table and knocked down two chairs. The bar was loud, and the brutal fight had turned the crowd rowdy. Nobody noticed how rough Jimmy handled Trudy's frame.

Meekly, Charles quietly sat down and smiled at Jimmy. He wasn't no fool; he was the one holding the money. He drank from a flask in his jacket. Though he felt bad for Trudy, he didn't want any trouble for himself. He stared at the TV like everyone else.

It was already round three. Liston stuck Jones against the ropes. Liston's bloated glove cut Jones across his jutting-out maw. Jones' skull turned a horrible Merlot.

Charles silently watched Jimmy twist Trudy's arm behind her back. He sipped from his flask as Jimmy slammed her into the men's bath-room. Charles bit his lip. He could taste the peach brandy. He looked up at Percy. Percy smiled down at Charles, daring him to move. Charles looked back at the set.

Jones broke from the ropes and snatched the battlefield back. In a blizzard of hits, he nailed shot after shot. Liston did a strange dance, like his legs didn't know each other. He swayed in a dull haze and almost went down. The crowd jumped from their seats and flew into a frenzy.

"Stomp his ass, man!"

"Bash Hitman's teeth!"

"We want to see that punk bleed!"

Jimmy grabbed a whole handful of Trudy's thin braids. An elderly man quickly zipped up and left when Jimmy slammed her against the cold tile.

"Now, I'm going to ask you, and I'm only going to ask once." Jimmy breathed hot, angry air in her mug. "Where the fuck were you today?" His hand was balled-up, his neck muscles bulged and her braids were wrapped tight around his fist.

Trudy panicked. Her air passages felt closed. She took quick, panting breaths. Her eyes darted back and forth but no one else was in the room. She wished someone would come in and help.

Suddenly the whole place filled with loud, whooping screams. Liston left-hooked Jones in the rib cage and chin. Liston kept drilling Jones with heart attack jabs, hammering him with swift combinations to the head and the body. When a right jab caught Jones smack-dab in the eye, the weak tissue ripped and people went crazy. The cut man had a hell of a time stopping the ooze.

Jimmy's veins bulged like snakes slithered under his skin. His red face was tense with hot venom.

Trudy held her mouth shut. She decided to stay quiet. She was afraid if she said something, uttered one small wrong word he'd slam her face into the glass.

"Talk to me, girl! I asked you a question." Jimmy tightened his grip around Trudy's long braids. "Where the fuck were you? I drove by your place twice. Tony ain't seen you all day."

Trudy struggled not to cry. She had to think of some lie that would stop Jimmy's rage, but her whole brain was numb and her skull really ached from him yanking her hair. Her scalp felt like it was inflamed.

"You in this, huh?" Jimmy slapped her face hard.

Trudy shook her head no. Her lids brimmed with tears. She struggled to stop them. To not let one drop. This was just how she felt when confronted by her mother. Her mother would scream and yell right in her face while Trudy willed herself not to weep. She knew if she let one fall, let one single drop, her whole face would flow like an ocean.

Jimmy let go of her hair and took a step back.

Trudy took a half breath when she saw Jimmy

smile. It took everything she had to try to appear calm while her insides raged on like a storm.

"Come on, baby, it's me, Jimmy. I wouldn't hurt you, girl."

Jimmy smiled at her cunningly while he pulled out his gun. He wiped the gun clean with a white satin cloth. He spoke to her softly, saying each word nice and slow.

"Now I'm going to ask you one time." Jimmy folded the cloth, putting it back in his pocket. He was standing so close she could count the lines in his eyes. Jimmy aimed the clean gun against the hollow of her throat.

"Tell me everything and you won't get hurt."

Trudy wouldn't speak. She just stood there silent. She tried to breathe easy as her blood blazed with fear. She was losing the fight in trying to stay calm and was almost engulfed in full panic.

Trudy's mind flashed to the only time she ever got caught. It was two years ago and she hadn't stolen in weeks. She was desperately trying to stop. But before she left this store she saw a beautiful jacket. It was lavender suede with a furry fox collar. She looked around the store without moving her head. She quickly unlooped the big metal ring and pulled the chain out through the arm. She glanced around the store again. She slipped the coat on. She casually took the escalator downstairs while the fluorescent lights shined on her brow. She could see the front door. She saw the cars in the lot. When she finally got both feet all the way out and inhaled deep, someone violently grabbed hold of her arm. Trudy was shocked. The undercover came from nowhere. She'd never seen the man anywhere near her in the store.

"Come with me, miss," he said, holding her firmly. He brought Trudy to a small basement room. A man behind a desk asked her all sorts of questions. "Who are you with? Where are your parents? Don't you know stealing's a crime?"

While sitting there still, Trudy unzipped her purse. Her body was rigid. She just moved her hands. Her fingertips searched through her purse for her wallet. When she found it, she lifted her pants leg with one hand and shoved the wallet inside her boot.

Trudy was eighteen. She did not want to go to jail. But taking a five hundred–dollar coat was considered grand theft. She had no choice but to lie through her teeth. "I'm only fifteen," she told him without blinking. "I thought you had to treat minors different."

"You're under age?" the man examined her hard. With her body and made-up face she looked at least twenty. "Hand me your purse."

The man grabbed her bag and dumped the contents on his desk. There was makeup, a mirror, a Mr. Goodbar and sixty-five dollars in cash.

Trudy knew as a minor she couldn't be charged, but the manager was pissed. He didn't like losing a suspect. So he called the cops to come down to the store anyway and take her. They cuffed her and took her back to the West L.A. station. Trudy was petrified riding in that black and white car. One cop rode in the backseat with her.

"Tell us everything," the nice cop said, "and you won't get hurt." He smiled with the warm face of a father.

"She's a thief," the other one barked. "Don't waste your time. I can't wait to lock her up in a cell."

The police jumped right into their Mutt and Jeff routine. She ignored the hard one driving and looked at the one who stayed nice.

"Tell us everything," the nice one said. "We'll go easy on you, honey. Is there anything you want to say? Do you have more stuff at home? How long have you been shoplifting?" he wanted to know. "Tell us and I promise you won't get hurt."

Trudy shook her head no. She blinked tears from her eyes. She tried to create a look that mixed sweetness with sorrow. She knew about Mutt and Jeff, the good cop, bad cop routine. She knew it was best to keep her mouth shut.

When they got to the station she looked on the floor. There was a thick yellow line, two out-lined feet and letters saying, STOP HERE AND FRISK.

Trudy was frantic. Were they going to frisk her right there? They would find her ID. They'd realize she was lying. Damn, she was going to get caught. But Trudy toyed with the cops, she asked them questions about their job, and when it was time to walk up to the frisk line and stop, the cops walked her right over the letters. They brought her inside the station. They joked with her more. Someone brought her a cold can of Sprite. They liked having this sexy young thing in the station and leered at her giant young breasts. She watched when they brought in a young-looking brother. He held her gaze for a second. They worked him over hard and threw him down inside a cell. Trudy watched the man standing, holding the dark steel bars. She was glad she'd kept her mouth shut. She'd always be grateful for what her mother did for her that day. Joan came to the station as soon as she got the call. Trudy didn't have to tell Joan she'd lied about her age. Joan came in and sized up the whole situation. In ten minutes she had gotten Trudy released. She scolded the cops for "hand-cuffing babies" and immediately took Trudy home. Joan never got after her about stealing that stuff. She thought getting handcuffed was punishment enough.

* * *

Trudy clenched her back teeth as Jimmy's gun pressed her neck. She knew one thing for sure: it would be worse if she talked. So Trudy did just what she did back then. She stood there and did not say one word.

When Jimmy realized Trudy was not going to talk, he cold-cocked her hard in the jaw.

Outside the bathroom door, the club went berserk. People were howling and screaming and hitting spoons against bottles. Jones left-hooked Liston in the ear. Liston looked stunned. He swung at the air. He tried to throw a right but his timing was off. He took a full swing but he missed and lunged forward, teetering back and forth on his water-hose legs. Liston was dazed, like someone who forgot where they'd parked, like any minute he'd be eating the canvas.

Trudy dropped to the floor. Her mouth tasted like salt. She could move her front tooth back and forth with her tongue. Trudy wished she could blast Jimmy's head with her gun, but her gun was in her purse on a chair.

Jimmy stood over her, putting one foot on her chest. "Look, I don't care. This can go either way. Just tell me where my cocaine is at."

He started choking her neck with his boot.

Just then Pearl burst through the men's bathroom door. Jimmy had one foot at Trudy's throat and aimed his gun straight at Pearl's face.

Pearl stopped in her tracks. She squinted

hard at Jimmy. She was wearing a long, silvery, sequined gown. One fist was hitched to her thick, strong, firm hip, and the other fist held the neck of a long wooden bat. She glanced quickly at Trudy but held a steady gaze at his eyes. Pearl stood like he could shoot her nine hundred times and she'd still be posed the same way.

Jimmy held the gun, but he dropped it a few notches. "Oh, I'm supposed to be scared." Jimmy laughed in her face. "Come on," he said to Pearl. "Go ahead, take a swing. I'll even put my gun down."

Jimmy loved this. This was big fun to him. He loved taunting folks. To him this was pure pleasure, like a kid stabbing bugs with a stick.

"You need to be clocking some of these fools up in here instead of wasting your time messing with her." Pearl threw a glance over her shoulder toward the door. "I heard someone came in here with a *whole* bunch of money. You need to go see about them."

"Who? What the hell are you talking about?"

"Tony knows. Ask him. He been bragging to anybody who'll listen, talkin' 'bout he got big bank tonight."

Jimmy pushed past Pearl and peeked from the door. Tony was laughing, sloshing drinks into rows of shot glasses. Both fists clutched two expensive bottles.

Jimmy looked confused. He clicked back his

gun and shoved it into his waist. He reached down and pulled Trudy up. "Look, I don't know what's up, but don't try to leave." Jimmy put his gun in the back of his waist. "You better stay put. I'm not done with you yet."

Trudy wanted to spit in his face.

Jimmy left the bathroom and went back inside the club. He told Percy to watch the bathroom door.

Trudy ducked inside the men's stall and pulled across the latch. She was so scared she almost peed in her panties. She watched Pearl from the stall's tiny crack.

Pearl hissed a sharp whisper when Trudy came out. "Girl, didn't I tell you not to tangle with him? That crazy fool don't need a reason to murder. That mean shit just runs in his blood."

Pearl narrowed her eyes as she peeked out the door. Jimmy and Tony were starting to yell. "Look, girl. I found it upstairs." Pearl handed her a wrinkled piece of paper. "I knew I'd find something if I kept snooping around."

"What is this?" Trudy said, scanning the sheet. "Looks like a receipt to a rest home in Barstow."

"Look at the name at the bottom," Pearl triumphantly said.

In tiny print at the bottom of the receipt was the small name "Miss Geraldine Dee."

"You mean Miss Dee's up there? She's been alive all this time!" Trudy could hardly believe it.

"That's just what it means, according to this.

That no-good dog lied to us all." Pearl looked out the bathroom door once again. Jimmy was talking even louder this time. Another man knocked down an older man's drink. Some women were screaming for shots. "You best get the hell outta here, chile. I smell a riot up in this spot tonight. Better use the side door in the back."

Trudy nervously walked toward the dressing room door when Percy left the bathroom door to pat some man down. Charles raced up to her elbow. He handed Trudy her purse.

"What happened in there? I was scared to come in." Charles meekly dug both his hands in his pockets.

"Um," Trudy said, rummaging around the junky room. Finally she found what she wanted. She took a hairy mass from out of a bag and shook the brown curly wig out. "Where's the money?" she asked Charles, watching him in the mirror. She shoved all her braids up under the wooly-haired cap and slipped on some dark tinted glasses.

"I got some of it on me," Charles said, opening his jacket, revealing the blue vinyl pouch.

Trudy quickly yanked Charles's jacket shut. "Are you crazy? Keep that thing closed. That fool almost killed me a minute ago! And what do you mean 'some of it'? You don't have it all? Charles, where the hell is the rest?" Trudy stopped peeking out from the dressing room hole, staring Charles in the face.

"I couldn't let Ray Ray see I had all that cash. I hid the rest."

"Hid what?" Shirley said, bursting through the small room. She surprised Trudy and Charles. They stood totally stiff, like kids caught making out in the closet. Shirley grinned wide, popping her gum. "Ummmmm! Whatchu all doing hiding in here, huh?"

Trudy impulsively grabbed Charles's hand.

"You something else, girl. Ain't no shame in yo' game. Don't matter to you if he's taken or not. You want some, you get some, you treacherous skank." Shirley rolled her eyes up and down Trudy's body. She popped her gum loud in her face. "I ought to tell your ol' lady myself," she told Charles. Shirley grinned at the wig sitting on Trudy's head. "Oh, hello! Are we role-playing tonight? You trying to be Cleopatra Jones in this bee-yatch?"

Shirley reached over and tried to snatch the wig off. But Trudy caught her hand and slapped it away. She was shaken and angry about what happened with Jimmy. She reached in her purse and pulled out the gun.

"Touch me again and I'll blast your jacked-up face," Trudy said.

Shirley was stunned. Her mouth dropped

completely open. She backed to the corner of the room.

Charles was stunned too. He didn't know Trudy had a gun. When she said "come on" this time, he did what she said.

Trudy and Charles pushed through the tight crowd of people in the club. Shirley watched them out of the dressing room hole. "I'ma get you for that, bitch. Don't think I won't." She blew a giant pink bubble with her gum.

"Walk slow but keep moving. Try and stay cool. We gotta get out of here fast!" Trudy's brown eyes slid across the dense, smoky club. It was packed with folks watching the loud, angry fight. "You go out front. I'll meet you in back." Trudy didn't see Jimmy. But Percy was there. He was obviously searching the room for her now. But Percy was looking for Trudy's long braided head; he didn't recognize her in dark lenses and brown curls. Trudy snuck out the back. Charles drifted out front. He trotted quickly toward his car.

Charles saw Trudy ease out the back door of Dee's. But she didn't rush over to Charles's car first. Instead, she raced over to a huge glossy black SUV and carefully sliced all four tires. Charles took another big swig from his flask, letting the warm liquor enter his skin.

Trudy raced toward Charles and jumped in his car. She gushed out a sigh of relief. Charles stroked her hair, touching the curls on the wig, which glistened in Dee's warm neon glow. Charles eased his brandy-stained mouth over hers but Trudy pushed Charles's face back.

"Uh-uh! Let's go! We gotta leave quick." Trudy breathed deep and exhaled out of the window. Homeboy was tripping, she thought to herself. She looked at Charles hard out of the corner of her eye. He was too scared to come in the bathroom to help her and she'd almost been shot in the face. Trudy cracked the window. She needed to breathe some cool air. Charles was testing her nerves.

"Where's the rest of the money?" Trudy urgently asked.

Charles's eyes shifted down the street. "It's at home. It'll be safe there."

"You left it at home? Where did you put it? How do you know it won't get stolen?"

"It won't. It's hid real good." Charles took out the blue vinyl pouch of money. "You want to have part of it now?" He could lie about what was left in the envelope now by saying the rest was at home.

"No, Charles, let's go. We can't do this here. We'll divvy it up at Vernita's." Trudy strapped on her seat belt.

Charles strapped his too. He decided not to say he'd given some of the money away. He was feeling euphoric. He'd paid Tony back. He was holding an envelope with some serious money and there was plenty more waiting at home. For the first time in a long time he felt like a man. He wasn't about to spoil his good mood by being honest. He tried to peck Trudy's cheek but she pushed him away.

"Let's go," Trudy said hastily.

That's okay, Charles thought. He drained the rest from his flask. He could definitely wait. He turned the ignition. He clicked the radio on and switched the headlights. He thought about the paint can with the money and smiled. He put his hand on the gearshift and adjusted his mirror. Trudy had the sweetest little worried look on her face. Like a child trying to figure out a difficult puzzle. But suddenly her face changed to horror.

Trudy screamed but before she could finish Charles heard the gunshots. Three loud, angry blasts. Trudy slowly sank into Charles's lap. Blood leaked all over her dress.

Flo stood at the car window. Her face was enraged. Her chest heaved up and back down again. The warm gun dangled limply from her wrist.

18

Ray Ray

When people heard those shots they started running outside.

Trudy thought she'd been shot when she finally eased back up. She thought she'd see Jimmy standing next to the car. But Jimmy wasn't there. He wasn't anywhere around. She lifted her head slowly to look.

Pearl was out first. "Somebody call the police. Hurry!"

People began to get in their cars and pull away.

Ray Ray looked around wildly. "What happened?" he asked.

"Get out the club, man. Police'll be here any minute." Sonny was about to go. Even Big Percy hurried away.

Ray Ray wasn't leaving. He scanned the club's

room. Chairs were turned over, bottles lay dripping. A large crowd of people tried to squeeze through Dee's door, like booze coming down through a funnel. But Ray Ray had business. He walked quickly upstairs. He wasn't about to leave the club without getting his money. He eased the door open to Tony's small closet office. Tony was stuffing something in a brown leather bag.

"Hey, Ray Ray, whatchu doing up here, man? Ain't you heard? A man down there's been shot. We got to clear out before the police gets here, boy!"

Ray Ray didn't move.

"Didn't you hear? Whatchu waitin' on, son?" Tony didn't even bother looking up. He hastily shoved some papers in a briefcase.

"Naw, man, I didn't hear nothin'. I got business up here. I ain't leaving without you giving me my money." Ray Ray's eyes locked on Tony. Tony's locked back on his.

"I done tol' you already, the man's got it. I passed it on to him. He got it now, got mines too. You saw him in here collecting all them bets. You give it to me and I give it to him, remember? I know you saw him. He came right over to where you and Charles was." Tony was talking real fast. He wanted to get his cash and get out.

"I didn't see shit," Ray Ray said flatly.

"Listen, man, Jimmy came in and took the bet money. We got to leave before the law turns the place out!" Tony stood up and tried to walk around Ray Ray's frame. But Ray Ray was blocking his path.

"I ain't leaving without my ends, man." Ray Ray took out the gun in his underarm holster.

"Come on, man," Tony said, laughing nervously now. "Don't do nothing rash. I'ma get you your money. You know I'm good. Don't I always come through? Didn't I treat you like a son? Wasn't I the one who hired your black ass when all of them other folks wouldn't have ya? Now put that gun down. Think about what you're doing. You don't want to go back to the pen."

Ray Ray walked closer. Tony felt his breath on him now. Ray Ray pressed the gun into his stomach. A ripple shook his gut like a rock tossed in a pond.

Under the small hanging light, Tony's worried face creased. His eyes darted around the room like a brown, scurrying rodent, hoping for some kind of opening.

"I'ma go in my pocket. Look, man, don't shoot." Tony slowly pulled a handful of hundreds from his pocket. "All right. See. Looka here. I got five hundred dollars. Take it. It's yours. You can have it all, son. Now come on, man, put the gun down!"

Ray Ray looked down at the sad wad of cash.

"You must be sick. Where's the rest of my ends, nigga? I played Jones to win. I ain't leaving without my eight grand." Ray Ray shoved the gun farther into Tony's fat stomach. Tony's whole face was dripping sweat now.

"Now, hold up, man, hold up! I done tol' you already!" Tony's eyes looked crazed. Sirens were blaring. He had to get out. "I ain't got it, I said! The man came and took all the cash. I know you musta saw him. I put it on Jones. Just like you said."

Ray Ray didn't say a thing. He raised the gun higher. Putting it right next to Tony's bald head, he pulled the safety way back until it snapped.

"All right, man! Okay!" Tony pulled a small briefcase from below the desk but didn't open it. He saw Jimmy coming up behind Ray Ray real quiet. "Let me get you your shit, before you act a stone fool." Tony unsnapped the case. It was stuffed full with money. "This is what I get hiring a damn convict." Tony slowly stepped back. "Here's yo' shit, man." Tony stepped farther back. "Go ahead, take it."

But when Ray Ray leaned forward to reach for the case, Jimmy grabbed Ray Ray's throat and snatched back the gun, pointing it back at Ray Ray's face.

"Be cool, man. Don't move," Jimmy whispered. "All I want to know is where is my stash. They said brothers jacked my man this morning at the bank. Said one was a tall, thin, pretty-boy type." Jimmy grinned in Ray Ray's scarred, scowling face. "Now that sho' ain't you." Jimmy continued to smile. "Naw, cuz you as butter-black ugly as they come."

Jimmy rolled the gun over Ray Ray's large, gravelly scar. He stood in Ray Ray's face and continued to whisper. "But my man said the other one had a nasty burn mark peeking out under his scarf." Jimmy took out a knife and ripped open Ray Ray's skin. Ray Ray winced. Jerking back, he clenched his back teeth. Dark blood rolled from his keloid. Ray Ray stood there in pain as the sticky blood seeped over his neck.

Tony walked up to Ray Ray and spit in his face. "Yeah, it was him. Dumb stupid convict. Came in today with a whole gang of money. I bet he and Lil Steve been plotting this shit all week. Lil Steve probably snatched your cut, man."

Jimmy socked Ray Ray's gut and he doubled over. "Where's my shit, huh? Where the fuck is it at?"

Tony closed the brown briefcase and put it under his coat. This wasn't his fight. He wasn't in it. He scurried down the stairs while the sirens grew fierce.

"Put both hands around your neck," Jimmy barked loud to Ray Ray. "Now, don't turn around or I'll blow your damn head."

"Open up," they heard the cops yell from downstairs. They were banging the wrought-iron door with batons, but they couldn't get the door to bust open.

Jimmy backed out of the room, aiming his pistol at Ray Ray. Jimmy didn't want to be caught at the club with the cops. He backed all the way out of the room and ran out the back door.

Tony didn't want the cops to see he had a gambling room upstairs, so he locked the gated door tight.

But the officers were prepared. Two of them held a battering ram. They hooked the ram onto the large steel door. With both of them holding the thick metal pole, they knocked the iron door off the hinge.

The police charged up the stairs with all their guns drawn. Ray Ray's eyes darted around the small closet he was in. He could hear their feet on the stairs. He couldn't go back to jail. He couldn't get caught.

"Please, Lord," Ray Ray said, rubbing the cross at his neck, "don't put me in that black hole again." Even though he was two floors up, Ray Ray broke a small window over a water heater with his gun. He said one last prayer and then jumped. His body was almost completely halfway out when someone grabbed his leg and dragged him all the way back.

"I got one," a police officer proudly announced.

Ray Ray was caught in a black uniformed knot.

The cops cuffed him quickly. His hands dangled in front. His silver cross glittered against his gray pinstripe suit. His dark suit was splattered with blood.

"That's him!" Tony said, walking back inside the room. He wasn't carrying the old briefcase anymore. He looked straight at Ray Ray. "Yeah that's the one who done it. I hired him to work. Didn't know he was a felon. He shot one of my best paying customers too."

"You a lie! You know I didn't shoot nobody!" Ray Ray said. He struggled to get free, but the officers held him firm. They dragged him downstairs and out the front door toward the blinking squad cars at the curb.

Ray Ray tried to resist, twisting and contorting his body. But once they got him on the sidewalk they beat Ray Ray down. Their batons smacked his arms, his rib cage and his legs. They beat him so hard on the back of his head, blood flowed from out of his nose. Jamming Ray Ray's dazed and doubled-over body into the backseat, they slammed the door hard and took off.

Ray Ray lay unconscious on the black vinyl seat while the car screeched down the dark street. His silver cross medallion dangled next to his face. It was a thick chain with a fat cross of Jesus. The officers didn't bother to take it. He was cuffed and inside the backseat metal cage. Ray Ray wasn't going nowhere but jail.

Ray Ray gradually regained consciousness. He opened his eyes. He looked around, trying to figure out where he was. The car was racing downtown. Ray Ray had trouble breathing. His ears were ringing loud and his nose was all caked with blood and he had to pry his face from the seat where Jimmy had opened his wound.

He looked up and saw the two officers' heads. They were cracking jokes and laughing and running red lights. They never once looked back at him.

Now, officers aren't supposed to handcuff in the front, but sometimes they get lazy. They let their guard down. Ray Ray knew one thing. He had two strikes already. He wasn't about to go back to the pen.

Ray Ray raised his cuffed fists and used the tips of his fingers to work the medallion he was wearing. The flat silver cross had four slender tips. He put one of the tips inside the narrow keyhole. He started fiddling the cross around and around with his fingers until he heard the gentle snap of the lock.

Ray Ray kept his head down. His eyes searched for an escape. But the backseat was as tight as a cage. He didn't want the officers to know he was awake or notice his free, uncuffed hands. He felt around the seat but came up with nothing. He checked the side windows but they didn't roll down. He looked under the floor mats and that's when he saw it. There was a dim light coming from the front seat.

There was an opening! A space wide enough for a shoe. Ray Ray dropped his whole head all the way down and saw the officer's boot on the ground. He stretched, reaching his hand as far as it would go. He grabbed hold of the foot and wouldn't let go.

The driver slammed the brakes hard but the car skidded toward the sidewalk. It jumped the curb and kept flying down the street, slamming into a dense concrete bus bench. The car dangled halfway on the curb and the road. The driver was knocked out and slumped over the wheel. The horn tortured the normally silent street. A Mitsubishi swerved and braked hard but couldn't stop. It smashed the police car with such a strong force it knocked the driver's door open. Ray Ray kicked his door window until he shattered the glass. He leaped out and grabbed the slumped officer's gun. He started running down the block. The other officer was conscious but dazed. He grabbed his gun and shot at Ray Ray but Ray Ray shot back. He clipped the officer in the shoulder.

Ray Ray raced down the street like a wild, rabid dog, hopping a fence and scaling two walls and then ducking into a beat-up apartment. He crept down into the apartment's garage and saw an old blue Ford pickup parked against the garage wall. Ray Ray popped the hood and examined the engine. He looked around the garage for a tool and spotted a mangled coat hanger on the floor. He wrapped his bandana around the end of the hanger. He touched the solenoid and the battery cable. The Ford engine roared to life. Ray Ray busted the window and leaped inside the truck. He sped down side streets until he reached the 110. Keeping his eyes on his rearviews, he opened the ashtray. He found half a butt and popped in the lighter, but Ray Ray didn't light up until he was all the way past Gage. Ray Ray knew one thing; he had two strikes against him and had just shot a cop. He'd best get out of the state. But as he drove, something gnawed him. It clawed at his gut until he couldn't shake that sick feeling away anymore. It was against his best judgment. He knew it was wrong. But Ray Ray made a U-turn and went all the way back.

19

Trudy and Charles

After Charles was shot, and before the cops arrived, Dee's Parlor was going berserk. People raced through the streets like they did during the riots. Some folks were screaming, and one man waved a toy gun. Others just went in and took what they wanted. They ran holding six-packs and bottles of gin. An elderly lady struggled with a big stack of plates. One dropped in the street but she didn't break her stride. She just hoisted the stack farther up her hip.

Trudy roared Charles's Buick down side streets and through alleys.

"Don't worry," Trudy told Charles's slumped-over body. "I'm going to take you to a doctor. We'll get you fixed up. Just sit tight and keep trying to breathe." But Trudy didn't take Charles to the hospital at all. She drove down the street until she got to her house. She wanted to pick up her black leather satchel and get rid of these old bloody clothes. But when she got near her block she made a U-turn instead. Was she crazy? It wasn't safe to go home right now. Jimmy might be waiting for her there. Charles's gas tank was on empty; the red light had come on. She couldn't keep driving for long. She parked behind a Dumpster in an alley to think. Charles's body slithered down in the seat. Flies were buzzing around the car on his side. Leaning him back up, Trudy sucked in her breath. The whole front of his shirt was drenched in red blood. Her white dress was splattered in rusty blood too. Trudy was frantic. Charles was hurt bad. She found a water bottle in the backseat and tried to give Charles a sip but the water just rolled down his chin. She ripped part of her dress to make a quick bandage. But the blood wouldn't stop coming out.

"Damn it," she said, beating her fists against the wheel. "I've got to get you to a doctor." Trudy raced through back streets, hovering at stop signs. There weren't many emergency wards anymore. She'd have to go down to King Drew. Trudy raced to the hospital and parked in the red lanes; she struggled to get Charles's limp body out. Grabbing his arm all the way over her shoulders, Trudy dragged Charles through the large sliding glass door.

But as soon as she came through the Plexiglas

door the alarm started screeching like crazy. Everyone stopped and looked at them both. Blood was splattered all over her dress. The bottom half was completely ripped off. Charles was so wobbly and weak, he barely could stand. Bright red blood soaked through most of his clothes. But it was late Friday night and this was "Killer King" Drew. The lobby spilled over with bullet and stab wounds. Some folks were worse off than them.

A security guard raced up to where Trudy was. Trudy panicked. Oh God, she was trapped. There was a guard waiting at the entrance to the lobby and a guard standing where she came in. She was captured inside a small plastic room. Everyone stared at her hard.

"Ma'am!" the guard barked. "Are you carrying a weapon?"

Trudy had forgotten about the gun in her purse. The gun had set off the metal detectors and the alarm brought out both guards.

"I have to take it, ma'am," the guard said, coming toward her. Oh no! Trudy began breathing hard. She didn't want to be arrested. What if they thought she shot Charles? What if they called the police?

"It's my husband's. He shot himself cleaning his gun. I begged him to not buy that thing. Please come take it away." Trudy kissed Charles softly on the cheek. "You'll be all right, honey. We're at the hospital now."

Trudy handed the officer the gun. He studied her awhile but eventually walked back toward the door.

A nurse handed Trudy a clipboard filled with forms.

"You got to see him now!" Trudy pleaded to the nurse. She wanted to get out of the room and away from the guards; they kept watching her from the front door.

The lady didn't look up at Trudy at all. She leaned over the counter and took Charles's pulse. She examined his wound. "He's breathing," she said. "The bleeding has stopped."

"He's bad off. You got to look at him now!" Trudy said.

"Honey, I got an arm sawed off, a drive-by that left eight people bloody and a hand ripped from fixing a disposal. Just take a number and please sit him down. I don't want no blood on my counter." The woman's eyes never left the chart she was holding. "We'll call you as soon as we're ready."

"A number? Is this a god damn butcher shop or what?" But when Trudy saw the hard looks of the other people waiting she quickly grabbed a number and sat down. There was a man whose hand drooped in a loose homemade sling. The fingers and thumb were completely chewed off. Blood caked in the folds of his skin. A pregnant woman twisted and turned in her seat. Her loud groaning echoed throughout the whole room.

Trudy looked around the room for two seats to-gether. A man with a gash in his leg moved down one. He sat next to a woman with a black and blue face.

When Trudy lifted Charles's jacket to cover him up, the blue envelope fell to the floor. Trudy opened the envelope to examine the contents. The envelope was more than three-quarters short. Trudy nudged Charles's slumped body.

"Charles, wake up," Trudy whispered in his ear. "Where is the rest of the money?" But Charles was groggy. Trudy shook his leg gently. "Charles!" Trudy said, more determined this time. Charles opened his eyes wide but then shut them slow. He groaned, folding his body in the seat. "Charles!" she said low, shaking his leg harder. The man with the gash looked at Trudy and frowned. The marred woman sucked her tongue and sadly shook her head.

But Trudy wanted to know. She had to find where he put it. "Charles, can you hear me? Charles, wake up!"

"Can't you see he's bleeding?" The man with the sling shouted. "Why don't you leave the poor fellow alone?"

Trudy crossed her arms on her chest and stayed quiet. She didn't dare say anything else.

"Ma'am!" the woman behind the counter calmly called. "The doctor will see you both now." A nurse came and helped Charles into a small curtained room. She swabbed his chest, took his temperature and left.

"Charles!" Trudy said, holding on to his arm.

Charles raised his head but then collapsed down.

The nurse rushed back in. "You'll have to leave, ma'am. He's lucky. It's only a flesh wound." She plugged in a monitor and thumped a syringe. "We'll let you know how he's doing," the nurse bluntly said. She yanked the curtain in Trudy's anxious face.

Trudy waited until the nurse left. She lingered way down the hall. When the nurse turned the corner, Trudy slipped back into his room.

"Charles!" Trudy whispered inside of his ear. "Where is the money? Where is it hidden in your house?"

Charles turned over. He opened his eyes. He started to mutter something but the morphine knocked hard at his door.

"Charles!" Trudy said, shaking his shoulder real hard.

"Get out," the nurse said sternly, rushing back in the room.

When Trudy refused to move, the nurse touched her arm.

"Charles!" Trudy said trying to hold Charles's shoulder. Charles was struggling. He tried to mouth a word.

"Paint," he said weakly. His lids fluttered and closed.

209

"Charles!" Trudy screamed at the top of her lungs.

The nurse tried to pull Trudy but she was frail and small. Her thin arms were no match for Trudy's big-boned girth. So she pushed a green button and set off the alarm. A buzzing sound consumed the room.

Well, this was it. This was her final, last-ditch effort. In a minute they'd be tossing her out the front door.

"Charrrrleees!" Trudy hollered. She let her voice roar. It carried like a *Ma Rainey's Black Bottom* song, thundering way down the hall.

A male nurse came in and grabbed Trudy hard but not before these words crept from Charles's slurring tongue.

". . . back . . . yaaaaa . . . rrrrrrd," Charles said. One eye was shut. "Paint can in garaaaaageeeee," he muttered, then passed out.

Trudy smiled big when she heard these last words. Even when the male nurse tossed her out of the double lobby doors, she grinned all the way to the car.

Less than five miles away, Shirley grinned too. She had followed Jimmy trying to drive on four flattened tires. She pulled alongside his black SUV. Her dinged Cougar rattled and choked at the light. She looked like an old carnival ride.

"Your left tires are gone." Shirley gestured toward his rims.

"It'll be all right," Jimmy said unfazed. His

tires were slashed but he could still drive. It was useless to put on his spare.

"I can help. I think I know who you're looking for, baby." She gave him a snaggletoothed grin.

Jimmy's black tinted window rolled the rest of the way down. He was angry as hell but smiled back at Shirley. He cracked open and lit a brand-new cigar.

"If you'da asked, I'da told you to not fool with that girl. Trudy thinks she's all that and a big bag of chips, but that girl ain't never been shit!"

Jimmy stared at Shirley. He wanted her to talk. "Where is she?" he asked her point-blank.

Shirley smiled and popped her gum for a minute. She wanted her last comment to sink in. The car parked behind started blowing its horn. Shirley waved the car to go around. Shirley rubbed her thumb and fingers together, gesturing she wanted money.

Jimmy stretched out his arm and handed her three new bills. Shirley rolled them and stuck the tube in her stuffed push-up bra.

"Thanks, sugar," Shirley said, chewing her gum fast. "If she's not home, then most likely she's down at Vernita's. It's a beauty shop off 10th, right on Mont Clair. I betchu that freak's over there."

Jimmy leaned halfway out of his large SUV. "How much you want for your car?"

Shirley popped her gum like a twelve-year-old girl. "I'll let it go for eleven hundred."

Jimmy peeled off more bills. "Here's five," he said hard. "Now get out before I take it for the three in your chest."

Shirley snatched the extra cash and handed him the keys. "Pleasure doing business," she said, popping her gum again.

Jimmy got in her Cougar and put it in Reverse. It clunked when he put it in Drive. But the Cougar was fast and it had a huge engine. Shirley screamed as he flew down the street. "Don't blink or you'll miss it," she continued to yell. "Lemme know if you need anything else!" She smiled as Jimmy's taillights faded down the dark block. Her cruel grin turned into a nastier scowl. She filed a few rough nails before walking down the street. "Serves that ol' skanky bitch right!"

20

Tony

Tony flicked the dead ash from his half-smoked Winston. His large walrus gut dug in the steering wheel he held. "Nigga shit," he said to himself. Tossing the cigarette butt out the window, he turned on Ray Charles and hummed. He kept glancing and checking and rechecking his mirrors as he drove the side streets back home. He pulled his Caddy up the narrow concrete strips of his driveway. In between the concrete strips was a long row of unmowed grass.

Tony carried his briefcase out toward the back porch whistling "Midnight Train to Georgia." He stopped and sniffed hard. Somebody was barbecuing something. He looked up and noticed the soft trail of smoke floating up into the black. Nobody could see inside Tony's backyard. It was completely covered with vines. The vines and trees grew in one dark, overgrown mass that twitched and screeched loud from the crickets and rats. Tony pried open the back step and lifted the plank up. With Ray Ray and Charles's money and the rest of the club's take he had more than eighteen grand in his hand. A grin inched its way from his thick bottom lip. "It's a crime to make this much scratch in one night." Tony laughed, flicking his Winston from his hand.

Before nailing the plank shut, he heard the Great Dane next door. It growled and barked through the hedge. Tony looked across the yard. It was totally dark. He could barely see past his own arm.

"Must be one of them opossums," Tony said to himself. "Always climbing across the damn clothesline and rooting through your yard." He hammered the one plank back down. If Tony had gotten up and examined it himself, he would have seen that the clothesline had been taken down.

When Tony stood up, someone hooped his fat neck. The cord choked him so hard, he couldn't get air. He struggled so furiously to get himself free that he kicked over a glass Sparkletts bottle. The Great Dane went crazy at the shattering of glass. It pounced against the thick chain-link fence and barked wildly. Tony's eyes bulged. His tongue was slung like a dog, a dog that's been run way too long. He wildly clawed against the tight fists that held him but the more and more he moved, the tighter the cord yanked until Tony's husky body went limp. His lungs fluttered once. His heartbeat slowed down. And his brain faintly played "Midnight Train" to him again before drowning in a galaxy of black.

Ray Ray unwrapped the clothesline from around Tony's neck. He took Tony's gun from his sack-of-rice stomach and dragged him to the fallen-down garage in the back. He put Tony inside an old trunk and locked it. He threw a thick rug over the top. People thought the smell was a hound that had climbed back there and died. It was months before anyone found him.

21

Trudy and Flo

Trudy hurried to Charles's car and jumped in. She studied the envelope with the money. She held the keys to Charles's house in her hand. She couldn't show up in Charles's car. Flo would recognize it in a minute. In fact, it wasn't safe for her to go over there at all. Flo probably meant to shoot her. Trudy ran to the phone by the hospital doors.

She dialed Vernita and listened to the phone ring and ring. "Vernita, pick up!" Trudy held the receiver to her mouth. "Come on, Vernita, be home!"

Suddenly the phone clicked. Someone picked up the line. "Vernita?" Trudy asked. "Girl, is that you?"

The person didn't say a word. There was only hard breathing.

"Vernita?" Trudy said in the receiver again.

"Hello," a voice said low. It was almost a whisper.

"Vernita, is that you? Why are you talking so low? I can barely hear what you're saying."

"Your boy's over here," Vernita faintly said.

"Who?"

"Who do you think? He's knocked out in my chair. I tied his hands with an extension cord. You better get over here quick."

Trudy drove to the shop. A black Bug was parked across the street. She searched Charles's car for some kind of weapon. She wanted something in her hand just in case. The only thing Charles had was a steering wheel lock. Trudy twisted the lock until the metal bar slid out. She lifted her dress and hooked the lock to her panties, letting the thick bar hang down next to her thighs. She couldn't see inside. The blinds were all drawn. Trudy gently knocked on the shop door.

"Vernita?" Trudy mildly called to her friend.

"Shhhh," Vernita said, unlocking the door. She held one finger up to her lips. "He's out but who the hell knows for how long."

Trudy looked by the rinse bowl and saw Lil Steve. He was snoring inside the salon chair.

Vernita noticed Trudy's stained and torn dress.

"Look, I don't even want to know what bullshit just happened. You're still breathing, so I guess you're all right. Just give me my share. I'm through with this mess. I'm not made for this kind of stress."

Trudy glanced away from her friend's pale eyes. "Uh-uh, not yet. I don't have it on me." Trudy studied the floor. She felt Vernita's piercing gaze. "We have to go get it from Charles's place."

"We? No, not me! I told you I'm done." Vernita pointed a manicured finger at Lil Steve's head. "That boy came here and held a damn gun to my head. I already helped you enough."

"But, Vernita, I can't go. Charles left the money inside his garage. Flo showed up at the club gunning for me and Charles. I just dropped him off at the hospital to get checked."

"See? That's what I'm talking about. I knew this would happen. This shit is foul. Look at you, you're a mess. You're covered in blood and Charles is at the damn doctor!"

Trudy broke down. She felt bad about Charles. Hot tears raced out of both of her eyes. Her frustration and the day's events finally took their toll.

Vernita handed Trudy a towel for her face.

"I knew it. I knew doing this wild shit was whack! Didn't I say this shit was crazy?"

Trudy struggled hard to pull herself together. "Vernita, I'm fine. Charles is okay too. The bullet went right through his shoulder, that's all. But I need your help. I just need a quick ride. I swear, I'll do all the rest."

Vernita frowned and didn't say anything at first, but her disgust made her yell at her friend. "That's all? Girl you must be sick! This is dangerous, okay? Your dumb ass could die! Have you been smoking chronic all night? This is idiotic shit. Look, I don't even care about the money. Y'all been shot at. Y'all coulda got done. Some of them gun fragments must have lodged in your head if you think I'ma still get in this fuckin' mess."

Trudy ignored her friend's sarcasm. She didn't have much time. "Charles told me the money is hidden inside a paint can. He hid the can in his garage. Look, I don't know why Charles put it in there but Ray Ray was with him. Charles probably had to hide it from him." Trudy held her friend's arm. She narrowed her eyes. "I got to get that paint can from Charles's backyard. All of our money is just sitting back there waiting. Vernita, we got to go before someone else gets there first."

"We? Haven't you heard what I said? Do I look like I got 'fool' written on my forehead?" Vernita's arched eyebrows rose high above her eyes.

"Come on, Vernita, please!" Trudy begged her friend.

But Vernita just stood firm. She didn't make a sound. Both hands were hitched to her hips.

"Come on, say something," Trudy demanded.

"I'm still thinking about that .22 glued to my jaw. I'm thinking about Flo tripping, getting a gun and shooting at folks. Why the hell would I want to go over there?"

"'Cause the money is there! Haven't you been listening at all? We got to go over there and get the shit back!"

"Naw, girl, I'm sorry. I'm not doing anything else. Guns, police, robbing banks, folks getting shot. And now I got this fool tied in my shop. This shit's way too deep for me."

Trudy stared at Vernita. Her deep frown was set. Trudy didn't know what happened between her and Lil Steve but Vernita was obviously scared. Trudy didn't dare say what Jimmy had just done to her. Vernita would never help if she knew the truth.

"Well, can't you just drive me over there, huh? I can't drive myself. I'm in Charles's car. Just drive me there. That's all I want."

Vernita sighed deeply. She wiped her hands on a towel. She grabbed some hair out of a brush and threw it in the trash. She placed a clean pile of combs in a large plastic jar. She filled the jar with green disinfectant. Her eyes shifted back up to the huge broken mirror. "I'm sorry. I just don't think it's smart." She grabbed a broom and started sweeping up shards. "You gonna have to be dumb by yourself."

"Look, I'm begging you, Vernita. Please help me out."

Vernita had heard enough. She turned her back on her friend. She scooped the glass bits and dumped them inside the trash. Her lips were drawn tight as she shook her head. "No, Trudy. I'm sorry. I can't help you now. I'm done with all of this mess."

So Trudy played her trump card. She had no other choice. There was one thing that could stop Vernita dead in her tracks. But she hated to use it. She'd sworn never to mention it again. But Trudy was backed against a cold concrete wall. "Wal-Mart," Trudy said. She let the word fall.

Vernita stopped sweeping. She clutched the broom in her fist.

"I know you don't want to hear it. I'm sorry to bring it up . . ."

Vernita flashed her green eyes. The white part looked red. She glared like she wanted to slap Trudy's face.

"I stood by you, remember? You *needed me* back then."

Vernita clamped her back teeth. She dropped the broom to the floor.

Vernita had buried that memory a long time ago.

See, in their last year in high school, way before Vernita had her own shop, Vernita worked for a beautician off 54th and Vermont. It was a small bootleg shop operating with no license, run by a mean, callous woman with thin lips and

221

a mustache. The callous woman came in demanding Vernita give her a perm. Vernita didn't want to do it. The woman's hair wasn't ready and it was dry and as hard as a broom. And on top of that, the woman had been scratching her head something awful and Vernita didn't want the perm to damage the woman's raw scalp. "Shut up," the woman said. "Just do your damn job. I'm not paying for your god damn opinion, okay? Just open that Revlon and start smearing it on. If you don't like it, then you can just quit!"

So Vernita got the jar from the shelf in the back. She told the woman to please have a seat in the chair. Vernita tied a smock around the woman's long neck. Vernita was careful not to get the harsh perm on the woman's skin, keeping the chemical just on her roots. But when she rinsed it, big chunks of hair came out in the comb and a whole lot more floated alone in the sink. The left side of the woman's scalp was completely skinned bald. When the woman saw her hair loss, she punched Vernita hard. Vernita got angry and slapped the bald woman back. But the woman went crazy. She tore up the shop. She cussed her; she pulled a razor blade from her purse, threatening to slash Vernita across the cheek. But just then, Vernita's young cousin Moon came in for a trim. Moon sized up the situation, which got immediately out of hand. A sea of tan khakis and white tees filled the room. Blue bandanas hung from their back pockets.

"Lock the door, cuz," Moon said to his friend. A tan-khaki man bolted the door. Moon slammed the woman hard against the wall. The razor fell out of her hand.

"You want to cut someone, bitch?" Moon spat in her face.

The half-bald woman panicked. She tried to run from the shop, but they caught her and dragged her inside their car. "Don't worry, girl, we got it from here." Moon gunned the car and careened down the street. "We 'bout to go do some shoppin'."

"Wait!" Vernita screamed. But the Monte Carlo didn't stop. The next day they found the woman's body inside a Dumpster. It was in the parking lot behind the new Wal-Mart.

When the cops questioned Vernita, Trudy covered for her friend. She told them she was with her all day at the mall.

"All right," Vernita said, finally leveling her eyes. "I'll do this last thing. But after this shit we're even. Don't ever bring that mess up again."

Trudy smiled at her friend. "I knew you'd come through."

"Look, Trudy, I'll take you. But I'm staying down the street. Flo might recognize my hooptie too."

"What about him?" Trudy looked at Lil Steve.

"If you help me we can lift him and carry him outside," Vernita said.

Trudy eyed Lil Steve tied up in the chair. She waved her hand across his face to see if he could see. She saw the cocaine in his nose.

"You think he ODed?"

"Naw, he's all right. Just strung out from being too high."

Sticking her hand inside his right pocket, Trudy pulled out a small ring of keys. They were both engraved with the Volkswagen logo. "Hey, let's use his car. That Bug out there's his. You're right. Your Mustang's too flossy to hide. No one will ever recognize us in a Bug."

Vernita looked worried but she still grabbed her purse. She took Lil Steve's feet and Trudy held his hands. They dragged him across the floor and outside to the back. Vernita locked up the shop when Trudy walked out the door. They walked around the corner and got into the car. Vernita turned the Bug's engine. She told Trudy to get down. Trudy smiled at her friend as she shifted from first. The Volkswagen roared like a Porsche.

As soon as they left, Jimmy appeared in the alley. He saw Lil Steve outside the beauty shop's back door. Lil Steve looked like a drunk who'd passed out in a stupor. As Jimmy got closer, something glowed in the moon. Jimmy eased the car closer to Lil Steve's body. He recognized the ring immediately. It was his diamond and sapphire pinkie. Jimmy got out and dragged Lil Steve inside the Cougar, spreading him across the backseat. He noticed a baseball bat behind the seat on the floor and decided to drive to the dark corner of a lot.

22

Trudy, Vernita and Flo

Flo went home feeling numb. She was driving half-conscious. "Oh my God," she said, gulping huge tears. "I can't believe it. Oh my dear God! I just shot my man!" She was going to open the car door and toss the gun toward the curb when a police car pulled up from behind. Flo made a right turn inside someone else's driveway and waited until the cop drove away. When she got to her house, she pulled the car to the backyard. She ran inside and bolted the front door.

Vernita downshifted to second and coasted through the yellow, revving the car loudly down the street. Trudy felt a large bulge under her passenger seat cushion. There was a ripped, jagged slash on the side. When she got to the next light she lifted her butt and pulled a duct-taped bag out. Vernita looked at Trudy while holding the bag. It was filled with a powdery substance.

"Oh, hell, naw! I knew this was wrong. We're in someone else's ride, driving with a whole gang of blow. Shit, I might as well drive us to jail right now and save some damn cop the trip." Vernita didn't want to go to Flo's house, and seeing that coke made her nervous. Vernita started to turn but Trudy held her hand. Trudy knew this wouldn't be good.

"Look, girl, don't trip. We're almost there now. Just ease up and pull down the street real slow."

"This was a fucking bad idea," Vernita told her friend. "Somebody gonna get hurt."

When they were three houses away, Flo burst out the door. She walked quickly down the driveway and out to the street.

Flo had put the gun in the bottom of a bag and was going to drop it down in the trash.

"Duck down—hurry, quick. Flo just came out!" Vernita shoved Trudy's head way down in the seat. Flo walked down the path with a small paper bag. She buried the bag down in the can at the curb.

"Vernita, stay calm. I know what to do. If she says something, you just talk to her, that's all. I'ma be right back," Trudy said. Trudy left the steering wheel club on the seat and quickly got out of the car.

Trudy slipped from the door, ducking down

between cars. She hid in a bush as Flo got to the sidewalk. Flo saw a Volkswagen idling a few houses down. She studied the driver. It looked like Vernita. What was Vernita doing driving a Bug? And why was she here on her street? Flo turned to leave but Vernita stuck her hand out and waved, so Flo walked toward her car.

"What are you doing here?" Flo asked nervously. She didn't know if Vernita knew she shot Charles or not. But she knew Vernita and Trudy were friends.

"Oh, my nephew just moved in down the street, guurl. I was bringing stuff to help him move in."

Flo looked questioningly at the empty backseat.

"Oh, I ain't moving no boxes." Vernita held out her hand. "I'm not breaking any of my nice nails, chile. Naw, I'm just bringing that little fool his car." Vernita watched Trudy out the corner of her eye. "That boy got me gallivanting all around town. I didn't know you lived right here." Vernita smiled wide, faking surprise. She saw Trudy running down Flo's long driveway and wondered if Flo still had the gun on her somewhere.

Flo faintly smiled. She tried to look normal. "Where's your Mustang?" Flo asked, avoiding her eyes.

"It's back in the shop. Girl, it's always giving

me drama. Cars are just like men, chile, some broke, some go too fast, all of 'em a pain in the ass."

"Well, I'll see you. I gotta get back in." Flo was eager to get back inside. Someone might recognize her as the shooter. She wanted to get off the street.

Vernita saw Trudy was just getting to the yard. "Flo!" she barked out.

"What?" Flo said, worried. *Oh no,* she thought, *Vernita must know something.*

"Girl, what in the world are you doing to your skin? I tell you your face is just glowing!"

Flo didn't feel like she was glowing at all. She did feel nervous. It made her feel clammy. But somehow she felt Vernita was bullshitting her now. She decided to bullshit her too.

"Girl, I don't buy none of them small expensive bottles." Flo grinned at Vernita. She showed all of her teeth. "All I do is just rub in some Crisco."

Meanwhile, Trudy was already inside the garage. It was an old cobwebby shack filled with all sorts of rubbish. Old coats and dead lamps and lots of beat-up boxes. A lot of odd paint cans were stacked on a shelf.

"Shit!" Trudy said out loud to herself. "How am I supposed to know which one it's in?" She started in the front, grabbing two of them down. But she had a hard time prying the rusty lids up.

Luckily she remembered she still had her keys. Her house key was the longest. She pried around the can, but when she tried to lift the top it bent her key back.

Damn it! She needed something stronger. She looked in the garage. It was murky and dark. She moved one of the boxes and then stopped in her tracks. There was an awful sound coming from the corner in the back. Trudy bit into her lip. She held her frame rigid. The clawing sound grew more intense. The sound would stop and then leap into wild, full-fledged scratching. Trudy was suddenly aware of a harsh animal scent. It smelled like a dog that'd been caught in a storm. Trudy was frantic with fear. Her eyes strained toward the sound. *I got to get that money. I've got to get out! Even if this garage is teeming with rats.* Trudy kept still. She studied her foot. If the rat ran across it she didn't know what she would do. A box stacked with books sat next to her leg. Trudy grabbed the one on top. She threw it toward the sound. The horrible clawing sound stopped. Frantically a small kitten flew out the garage door. Trudy breathed her relief. It was only a baby. She had to get a grip on her nerves.

Trudy opened a box, carefully sticking in her hand. But when she felt something furry she let go and screamed. The box dropped and all its contents fell to the ground. Trudy stood terrified against the spiderweb wall. The garage became murderously quiet. When she looked down she saw it was only a doll. The doll's long black hair spread out on the ground. Its dead blue eyes stared into hers. Trudy used her foot to kick the doll out of the way. She used her heel to sort through the rubbish. She was afraid to stick her hands into anything now. But next to the doll's gingham dress was another small box. It rattled with the hard sound of metal. The box was full of old tarnished spoons. Trudy grabbed one of the spoons and went back to the paint cans. She worked the spoon around the can and easily lifted the lid. But this first can was wrong. There was nothing inside but rancid liquid. The harsh smell stung the skin in her nose. Trudy grabbed the next can, but when she violently pried the sticky lid off, it dropped on the hard concrete floor. Trudy hoped no one heard the lid dropping sound. She waited, listening for the sound of someone coming. Trudy stared in the round can, determined to finish her search, but this one was filled with yellow two-toned gunk. "Shit! Trudy said reaching for the next can on the shelf but she stopped when she heard something, something like a twig snap. She stood mute. She was holding her breath. She peeked out the garage and saw the bedroom light on. Flo stood in front of the window. Trudy didn't move. She just stood quietly and waited. Trudy knew Flo couldn't see inside the dark garage. But she might decide to come out and check. When Flo clicked the light Trudy took a deep breath. She hurriedly pried the next paint lid. It easily slipped off. Finally, she found what she wanted. Glued to the white gunky can was a clear plastic wad. Inside the wad were thick stacks of cash.

Trudy emerged from the garage. She wanted to wash the paint from her hands, but the water hose nozzle was set to spray and the hose wet Trudy's whole face. She adjusted it fast, rinsing the slippery paint off and rubbing her hands on the lawn.

Flo was in the bathroom when she heard the sound of water. The old copper pipes started to groan.

Trudy ran down the driveway with the can in her hand. She didn't know if Flo was watching or not. All she knew was she finally had her hands on the money and she was getting the heck out of there now. As she ran down the street a lone car flashed its lights. She ran back toward the black Bug.

Flo got a flashlight and examined the backyard. Someone had been rummaging around in the garage and there was a white puddle of paint on their grass.

"Come on!" Trudy said. "Let's get out of here quick!"

Vernita had the engine going. She shifted to first. The Volkswagen skirted down the street.

Trudy started counting out money. She handed

a large wad to her friend. "Here, girl. That's yours. This is your cut. I threw in some extra 'cause you really helped me out."

Vernita couldn't believe she was seeing all this cash. The idea hadn't hit until the money touched her hand. Vernita raced down the street with a smile on her face.

"Drop me off two houses down. Let's stay low-key. I don't want anybody to see me come in."

When she got out Trudy scooted into the Bug's driver seat.

"So you headed to Vegas now?" Vernita said to her good friend.

"Yeah. But I have to stop in Barstow a minute first."

"Barstow? What the hell is up there?"

Trudy showed her the folded-up paper Pearl had given her.

Vernita saw the words "Rainbow Tree Rest Home."

"Miss Dee's up there. Can you believe Tony hid her up there? I'm going to check on her on my way out of town."

Vernita hugged her friend. She rubbed her big wad of cash. "I must admit. I definitely had my doubts. Who'd-a thought you could really pull this fucking thing off?"

Vernita patted her stomach. That's where she'd put her money. Her panties held the wad snug against her warm skin. The thrill of having all this money began to sink in. "Woowee, this sweet cash sure makes me feel good. It was a lot of trouble but I guess it was worth it."

"I told you don't worry. Didn't I say it'd be okay?" Trudy grinned at her friend and her friend smiled back. "Hey, maybe I'll send you a postcard."

Trudy revved the engine. "I better get going." Trudy held her friend's gaze for a minute. "I'll never forget you helping me, girl."

"Well, let me know, homechick, if you need me again." Vernita smoothed the small hairs on the back of her neck. She looked radiantly happy. Her bright green eyes shone. She was relieved. This crazy shit was finally over. She kissed Trudy's cheek and teetered back to her house. Her high heels smacked the rough concrete. But when she got to her door her wide smile dropped. The fine lines of worry began inching around her mouth. What about Lil Steve? What was she supposed to do now? The money didn't seem to offer much protection from him. She wished Trudy had asked her to go away with her. Staying here alone felt dangerous now.

23

Vernita and Jimmy

Vernita pulled the wad out of her panties once she got in the house. While keeping the light off, she studied the small room, wondering where she could hide it. She settled on the ceramic water jug in the kitchen. Lifting the three-gallon jug up off the base, she drained half the water in the sink. Vernita laid the plastic wad of cash down in the base, placing the half-full water container back on top.

"Lord," Vernita said, "I'm glad this shit's done." She turned the hot water faucet on in the sink until it flowed nice and warm on her skin. Emptying a small amount of shampoo into the palm of her hand, Vernita began washing her short, spiky hair. Vernita liked to wash her scalp whenever she felt stressed. It cooled her down

and made her feel refreshed. She took off her
blouse and put on a light robe, laying a towel
around her small neck. Lathering her head
until her whole scalp was nice and foamy, she
closed both her eyes, letting the warm water
flow as she slowly massaged in the soap. The
rushing warm water felt so good and relaxing.
Vernita let the water beat the base of her neck.
With her head under the spigot and her eyelids
shut tight, someone suddenly seized her and
held down her head.

A hand grabbed Vernita's mouth. Another
held her crown. The sink basin rapidly began
filling with water. Drumming her ears like a hot
sloppy tongue, the warm water killed off all
sound. Vernita struggled. She fought with all
her might to rise, but the hands forced Vernita
back down. The soapy water hurt her eyes. The
soap stung her nostrils. But not getting any air
inside of her lungs made Vernita's body twist
wildly with panic. Though she fought and she
strained, her arms flailing around, there was no
way to get any air. The hand left her mouth and
pressed her face against the bottom. Vernita
thrashed away and screamed. The rising water
surged with hostile bubbles. Vernita tried to bite
the hand but it was clamped around her jaw. She
twisted, she kicked the wood cabinets under the
sink, but she couldn't get the hand off her neck.
Vernita began to feel herself growing weak. Her
rubbery legs started to buckle. The water in her

nose seemed to ease into her brain. With her eyes open wide she could see only gray. Her arms dropped. Her heartbeat grew faint. As the gray world began to grow darker and turn black, the large hand lifted her back out. The hand pushed her against the washing machine. All the neatly stacked clothes dropped silently to the ground. Vernita began to choke uncontrollably loud. She ripped open her eyes and looked around the room wildly. Someone was holding her from behind. Jimmy stood a few inches from her eyes.

Jimmy took the moist towel and wiped Vernita's cropped head as the other man held her wet body.

"Thought y'all was slick." Jimmy said, glancing at the jug and then back in her eyes. "Where's Trudy, huh? Where the fuck is my stuff? What'd you dumb bitches do with the rest?"

Vernita was stunned. Water leaked from her lips. Jimmy held his gun while another man held her body. The man clutched her hard in a rib-crushing vise.

"You a cute little thing," Jimmy said, eyeing Vernita's slim frame. "I like a little more meat on, myself." Jimmy grabbed the back of her neck.

Someone held Vernita's arms tight, pulling them way behind her body, which lifted her breasts up a few notches.

Jimmy took a knife from out of her drawer.

He cut the robe's sash, revealing a lacy turquoise bra. "It'd be a shame to mess up something as pretty as this."

Jimmy lit a cigar. He watched Vernita's worried face.

Vernita strained and the hand eased up a little. She could see the slight hint of a slender goatee. It was Lil Steve! His jawbone looked funny. The bottom looked unhinged, and it was horribly swollen and bruised.

Jimmy took the sharp knife and cut open Vernita's bra. Her small breasts now stood completely exposed. Jimmy ran the knife point across the tip of one nipple. He began kneading and squeezing the other exposed breast like a kid playing in wet sand.

Jimmy stopped, whispering inside Vernita's warm ear. "Tell me where your friend is and I swear I'll stop."

But Vernita stood mute. She didn't say one word. Her eyes pleaded with Lil Steve. Why didn't he do something? But Lil Steve couldn't look Vernita in the eye.

He realized she must have been working with Trudy. She'd tricked him, although he wasn't sure how. He couldn't even look in her face.

Jimmy forced her head back in the water again. He held her so long she felt like she was dying. Water enveloped her nose and her lungs. She frantically fought against his hands.

When she rose again, Vernita was sputtering badly. She choked but could not catch her breath.

Jimmy stared in her eyes. He wiped her face with a towel. "Now, I know you don't want me to do that again."

"I swear!" Vernita screamed. "She didn't tell me shit!"

Jimmy grabbed her head and bashed her face to the sink.

"Wait! Trudy took Charles to Watts. They went to King Drew after Charles was shot. I swear to God, that's all I know!"

But Jimmy wasn't convinced and ducked her back underwater, holding her face all the way to the porcelain base.

Vernita struggled and thrashed, bubbles rose to the top. Though she fought Jimmy desperately and strained hard to breathe, her brain was beginning to grow numb. Vernita watched the swirling water upside-down in the sink. She wanted to live. She tried hard to speak but all the words came out garbled. There was no way to talk underneath all that water. Everything turned a dull, scummy gray.

Jimmy stopped plunging and lifted Vernita back up. As she rose she took in a lung full of water and suds. When he brought her up again, her skinny legs buckled. She fell to the cold kitchen floor and passed out.

Jimmy straddled her, pressing against her

small chest and heaved, pushing the water back out of her lungs. He wanted her alive enough to get what he wanted. He blew in her mouth while pinching her nostrils. He jammed his hands against her chest again and again until her blurry green eyes fluttered wide.

"You like swimming, huh? Ready for round three?" he joked. A cruel smile creased the skin around the corners of his eyes. "But I don't know. I had trouble bringing you back. You may not wake up this time."

"Barstow . . ." Vernita muttered as water rolled from her nose. "The Rainbow Tree Rest Home in Barstow."

Jimmy grabbed the phone and dialed information. "Yeah, Barstow. You got a Rainbow Tree Rest Home over there?" Jimmy smiled and wrote down the number.

"Now see," Jimmy said, standing, "wasn't that easy?" He picked up his coat, keys and fat, steely Glock. He took the money from the jug and put it in his coat pocket. He stopped, taking one last look at Vernita. He picked up her purse and walked toward her front door. But when he got to the door Jimmy abruptly stopped and turned. He shot Vernita right in the stomach.

Lil Steve was sick. He couldn't believe Jimmy had shot her. He doubled over and vomited on the cold tile floor.

"I told you I'm getting to the bottom of this

shit. The only reason you alive is I need you to get me Trudy and that ugly burnt fool you roll with." Jimmy lit his cigar and stood in Lil Steve's face.

"Here," he said, shoving Vernita's purse in Lil Steve's hands. "This shit may come in handy."

24

Trudy, Ray Ray, Lil Steve, Jimmy and Miss Dee

Trudy drove through the flat, empty desert for hours. She was hungry. Her red eyes were starting to burn. She desperately wanted to rest. The events of the day kept flashing through her mind. She had one last stop to make before escaping the state, and that was going to see Miss Dee in Barstow.

She pulled out the receipt and double-checked the address. She slowed toward an old beat-up, sloped-rooftop complex. RAINBOW TREE REST HOME, the crusty sign read. There was no tree in sight. The landscape looked vacant. The sad, aging building lacked any sign of color.

From the fence to the stucco, to the old chipping trim, was the same moldy, trying-to-hold-on beige.

Trudy grabbed her purse and got out of the car. Her open-toe shoes lapped up the dry sand. It ground against her toes as she hurried to the front door.

Jimmy hovered by the side of the rough desert road. At ninety-eight miles an hour he'd made really good time. He parked Shirley's old Cougar near some Joshua trees. They leaned in the olive-dim moon.

It was three in the morning when Jimmy lit his cigar.

"There's the car right there." Lil Steve pointed to the black Bug. Jimmy blew the smoke slow and looked at Lil Steve. "Remember what I told you," he said, pulling the latch. "Do exactly what I said or I'll blast off your dick. I'm not fucking with none y'all no more."

Jimmy ground his cigar right next to the car. He pressed his face up to the Bug's dirty window, looking down at the empty vinyl seat. He looked around the lot until he spotted a huge rock. He smashed the rock into the Volkswagen's window, reached in and pulled open the latch. There were some old bloody clothes and a white empty paint can. Lil Steve said the stash was inside the seat cushion. Jimmy pushed his hand all the way into the ripped slit but didn't feel anything there.

"Where the hell is it? You said in the seat!" Jimmy slammed Lil Steve back against the Volkswagen.

"I don't know." Lil Steve said, scared. "That's where I put it. She must have taken it out."

Jimmy glanced toward the Rainbow Tree Rest Home's front door. He let go of Lil Steve and popped his suit collar. Pulling the Glock from his waist, he carefully clicked in the clip.

Peering inside the misty glass doors, Jimmy looked inside the small rest home's lobby. The lobby was empty. There was no one in sight, so he pulled the cold handle, opening the heavy door wide, and shoved Lil Steve inside.

As soon as he walked in, he wrinkled his nose. The whole rest home reeked with the dense smell of piss. It was mixed with the powerful, harsh scent of bleach and the godawful stench of rotten skin. Jimmy took a small hanky and held it close to his nose, examining each room lining the beaten gray wall. This had to be the worst rest home he'd ever seen. Old people lay still on raggedy cots. Some of the twin beds had two people crammed in one. They watched Jimmy and Lil Steve with dull, hazy eyes. Thin, papery skin held their skeletal bodies. They all looked two heartbeats from death's door. Some had mouths hanging wide, some of them drooled, but others had chapped lips with crevices so deep they were caked in dried blood, like a riverbed that hadn't seen water in years.

Jimmy looked in each room, inching his way down the hall. When he turned the right corner he found what he came for. Trudy was leaning over this tiny, decrepit old woman. The old woman's once-braided plaits were now two fat dreadlocks. Loose, coarse hair sprung over the top. She was wearing an old, stained pair of men's pajamas. Another bony woman's face lay near her toes.

"Are you her kin?" the bony woman hoarsely said. Her voice sounded like someone shaking a big bag of rocks. "I knew someone would come. I been laying here praying."

Miss Dee tried her best to scoot up a bit but ended up slumped farther down. She seemed to be held by a string of IVs, like some old, worn-out, paper-thin puppet. A lunch tray with soup sat on a stand near her lap. And although a lone spoon slept on a napkin, her blotchy rheumatoid hands looked too gnarled to hold it.

"Oh, Miss Dee!" Trudy said, eyeing Miss Dee's wasted body. "Tony lied. He said you were dead!" When she leaned over to give Miss Dee's face a kiss, the bony woman's feet lying next to Miss Dee's head gently grazed Trudy's face. When Trudy felt those cold toes, she quickly pulled away. The toenails were ridged and completely curled in.

Miss Dee couldn't speak. A stroke had stolen her voice, but her twinkling eyes never looked more alive.

"I'm Agnes," the bony woman said. "She used to be down the hall but they put her with me month before last. Had a bad stroke and can't talk no more."

Miss Dee's face muscles rippled, trying to manage a smile. Her mouth was drawn and her skin was so deeply lined she looked like a plum left to rot in the sun. Her muscles were pulled so tight at the lip, it looked like a new baby's fist.

"My people don't never come visit me neither. But I knew someone would come. I told her I could feel it," Agnes said.

Miss Dee smiled again and grasped Trudy's hand. But as suddenly as the smile had appeared on her face, it immediately changed to pure fear. A tall man loomed behind Trudy's shoulders, but that's not what made Miss Dee yank the blanket over her face. Miss Dee hid when she saw the gun pointing at them from the door.

"Hey, girl," Lil Steve said low. Although it hurt when he talked, he managed a smirk. "Bet yo' ass is surprised to see me." Jimmy stood hidden in the rest home's dark, gloomy hall. Lil Steve knew he was pointing a gun at his back, and a line of perspiration made its way along his jaw.

Trudy jerked her head up and lurched toward the corner.

"I must admit," Lil Steve stepped closer, "you

had us all going. I didn't see none of this shit coming." Lil Steve chuckled. He did his best to appear friendly. But he kept smoothing the hairs on his mustache and goatee. Sweat rolled down to his ear.

Trudy inched farther back but there was no place to hide.

"You pretty slick, homegirl. Your game was real tight." Lil Steve clapped twice, miming applause. Now he was only a few inches from her face. "But quit trippin'. We don't need to play *Law & Order* no more." Lil Steve smiled inside Trudy's growing wide eyes. "Just give me the stuff back and I'll get it to Jimmy; then all this bullshit will be over." Lil Steve tried to act cool, but his worried eyes were pleading. He hoped Trudy listened. She better have that stash. He knew it would be over for him too if she didn't say where she hid the cocaine.

Lil Steve inched closer. Trudy felt his breath. "It's just you and me, baby. Ray Ray's in jail and Vernita is dead. You don't want to end up like them two."

Trudy looked at him in horror. This couldn't be true. "You're lyin'. I just saw Vernita, she's fine!"

"Well, I'm telling you, that nigga ain't playin' no more. Homeboy gunned her down. Executioner's style. Shot her point-blank in the dome," Lil Steve lied.

Trudy looked confused. This couldn't be

true. "Well, then, how come he didn't kill you?" Trudy asked.

Even Jimmy had to smile when he heard Trudy say that. She was as sharp as a tree cutter's ax.

"I know you ain't willing to die for some ends!" Lil Steve grew impatient with her now. He shoved Vernita's purse into Trudy's hands. "Look at that and tell me if I'm lying or not. Come on, Trudy! Just give the shit back!"

Trudy examined the purse and looked back at Miss Dee, who had pulled the blanket up to her eyes. This was definitely Vernita's purse. This was all of her stuff. Maybe Lil Steve was telling the truth. Trudy's whole body began filling with dread.

"Trudy, we don't have to go out like them," Lil Steve pleaded.

"Vernita?" Trudy asked. "Vernita's been killed!" Trudy felt so bad, she fell against Miss Dee's bed. But in the metal overhead light she saw something funny. A hand with a gun was right there in the hall. Lil Steve was setting her up.

"So what do we do now?" Trudy asked, stalling for time. Her eyes scanned the small room for some kind of weapon. But the only thing she saw was a paper towel holder on the wall and some antiseptic spray next to the food tray.

"Where's the coke?" Lil Steve demanded. He was really getting mad. He didn't like having that gun aimed at his spine. "Get the shit now and let's go!"

Trudy acted like she was about to go out the door. But instead she grabbed hold of Miss Dee's metal lunch tray and smacked it into Lil Steve's face.

Lil Steve yelled out in pain as the soup splashed in his eyes. The blow's impact killed his raw, throbbing jaw. Jimmy leaped, waving his gun, but Trudy held up the can. She sprayed the antiseptic right in his eyes.

With his eyes burning, Jimmy could barely see straight. He shot wildly around the room. Shots hit the ceiling and walls. There was a horrible, animal-sounding, blood-curdling yelp, like a mutt being struck by a car. But the yelp wasn't Trudy and it wasn't Miss Dee. Poor Agnes's head tilted down on her pillow. Blood oozed out of her nose. A bullet pierced through Agnes's neck. Miss Dee lay in fear. She couldn't do a thing. A lone tear rolled down the cracks of her face.

Trudy backed away toward the room's narrow corner. She was totally trapped. There was no place to hide. She felt like a roach underneath a huge shoe.

Jimmy grasped and held Trudy's quivering neck. "Where's the shit?" he screamed loudly. He was sputtering with rage. "I'll kill your whole fucking family if you don't tell me something quick!"

"I don't have it!" she screamed back. Trudy was scared out of her mind. She knew if she told him he'd kill her and be done. There was nothing else to do but try to stall.

"You a liar!" Jimmy spat. "Where's the shit at?"

Trudy tried to slither behind the IV and table but her foot got tangled inside the long see-through cord and the table crashed down to the floor. The IV ripped right out of Miss Dee's papery arm. A trail of dark blood flowed from her wrist.

During the blasting, Lil Steve dove to the floor. He inched toward the hallway, crawling on hands and knees. He figured it was best to get out if he could. He definitely didn't want to get shot.

When the table crashed down, Jimmy loosened his grip. Trudy grabbed the IV, dripping its clear liquid and rammed it inside his neck. Jimmy screamed in her face. He shot two more times, but they blasted the ceiling because he shot while snatching the needle from his skin, and the tall steel pole that was holding the IV came tumbling down on his back. At that point, Trudy scrambled and managed to get out of the room.

There were only two attendants working the late shift that night and one of them was out on his break. When the other attendant heard those gunshots coming from down the hall, she stuck her wet mop inside the bucket and left. The attendant snuck in a patient's room and ducked all the way down. She wasn't about to get herself shot on the job. Not on the bullshit minimum wage they paid her.

Trudy was almost at the front door. In a couple more steps she would be outside. It felt like it did when she'd shoplifted something, only a hundred and fifty times worse. Her heartbeat was pounding, her blood began to steam, and it was difficult to take a good breath. She put her hand on the handle, and the night air rushed in. She was almost there now. Her arm cleared the threshold. But just when her feet reached the darkness outside, just when she'd gotten her whole body out, just when her lungs finally took in some air, Jimmy hooked his thick arm around Trudy's waist and yanked her all the way back in. Trudy twisted and screamed but he had her this time. He slammed her so hard against the old stucco wall that the paint flecked down over the floor. The force was so strong she felt like she'd been whiplashed. Jimmy brought her down, clutching both her wrists, nailing her against the hard floor like Jesus.

"Where's my shit?" Jimmy yelled. His sweat dripped on her forehead. But Trudy's lips didn't move, though they trembled a lot. Her tongue stayed lodged in the roof of her mouth.

"Oh, you ain't talkin'?" Jimmy sneered at her face. He snatched a shank out from the back of his pants. He cut Trudy's hoop earring straight from the lobe. A piece of pink meat was still attached to the gold back.

The sight of her own blood immediately made her feel nauseous. But Trudy's mind was set. She clenched her back teeth. She turned her whole brain into a strong steel vise. Vernita was dead. Ray Ray was gone; she'd be damned if she talked to him now. And even though her concrete eyes were desperate to cry, she willed the hot tears from escaping down her cheeks. Jimmy read the determined look in Trudy's hard eyes. He put the knife back and pulled out his Glock. Jimmy was a pro at breaking folks down. He lived for this kind of challenge. He slammed the cold gun upside Trudy's face. Explosions of pain flared all over her skull. He hit her again and blood drained from her lips, then he jammed the gun under her teeth.

"Gimme my shit or I'll mess you up for life. No man'll ever look at you twice!"

The pain was intense. Trudy struggled to think. But her mind said she'd die before giving him what he wanted. She was alive only because he needed her to talk. Her whole body became a tight steel pipe.

Jimmy's face scowled crazily. He breathed heavy and deep. Trudy felt his foul breath warming over her forehead. But then something crossed over his hard, ruthless mind. Something made his cruel lips almost curl to a smile. He dragged Trudy down, pulling her along the long hall. He yanked her back into Miss Dee's narrow room. The white sheet under Miss Dee had turned a deep crimson. Agnes's blood was all over the bed.

"I'ma give you something to make your quiet ass talk."

Jimmy aimed the gun over Miss Dee's shrunken frame.

"Wait!" Trudy screamed, but it was too late for that. Jimmy fired the gun straight into Miss Dee's spindly thigh. A raspy growl erupted from Miss Dee's parched throat and ricocheted down the hall.

"Oh God!" Trudy screamed. "I'll tell you, please stop!"

Jimmy held the gun over Miss Dee's concave chest. Miss Dee's face was knotted. It rippled in pain. Her pleading eyes focused on Trudy.

"The car!" Trudy screamed. "It's all in the car!"

"I been in the car and didn't see jack." Jimmy's finger tugged the trigger and almost fired again.

"It's there, Jimmy, I swear. Check the right side. I hid it inside the door panel."

Jimmy smiled when he heard Trudy say this last part. So that's where it was. This was one clever heifer. It was too bad she tripped out and stuck him like this. He and a cold bitch like her could have worked something out. Jimmy jammed his Glock up against Trudy's rib cage. He hustled her down the hall toward the door. A bucket and mop sat next to the wall.

Trudy kicked over the bucket. Water splashed across the floor. Jimmy's Stacy Adam boots slipped in the murky, soapy water and Trudy managed to pull away. Jimmy shot wildly at her big legs but missed. He put a hole in the wall and another in the counter. When a bullet hit the sharp spokes of a wheelchair in the hall, the wrinkled-up man in it smiled. He patted the lumpy pacemaker under his shirt. This was the best shit he'd seen in years.

Trudy was free. She leaped to the door. But suddenly her whole head and neck were snapped back. Jimmy had a fist full of her braids in his hand. Trudy heard the cold first click of the safety go off as Jimmy pulled back the trigger. Trudy couldn't even struggle. She was caught and held tight. With his fist at her head, Jimmy dragged her outside. Trudy saw the broken glass outside the VW's door. Jimmy reached in and yanked open the driver's door handle. He snatched the inside door paneling off. The money and cocaine were lodged down in the metal.

Jimmy let the tip of his finger trace the edge of her face. He actually felt bad. He hated to have to kill her. For a second his hard face revealed tenderness inside. He had liked Trudy. She was all right. But then Jimmy's face changed. The gentleness quickly turned sullen. He examined the coke and thumbed through the money. He stared back at Trudy with felonious eyes. The savage eyes of the betrayed. She didn't want him. All she wanted was his money. His index finger hooked the slim trigger of his gun. He pulled the gun's trigger back.

Trudy closed both her eyes and held in her breath. The blast was so intense the Bug's window blew out. Trudy stood frozen, unable to breathe. When she finally decided to open her eyes, Jimmy's large body was slumped on the ground.

Trudy panicked. It was getting harder to get air. She looked around but saw no one in sight. Her eyes drifted around the black desert night and the red sea of passing cars. Suddenly, Ray Ray's smiling face walked toward the car door.

Ray Ray rolled Jimmy over and took Jimmy's gun. He held two fingers at his neck to check for a pulse before sliding his own gun back in his holster. He found the bag holding Vernita's cut of the money. He found a metal container with two new cigars and put it inside his jacket. He grabbed Trudy's hand, lifting her up.

"Hey, girl. You okay?" He noticed the blood on her shoulder and her earlobe cut off. Ray Ray brought Trudy back into the rest home.

Ray Ray rummaged through a drawer and found alcohol and gauze. He swabbed Trudy's face and her badly cut ear. He covered the lobe with a bandage.

Trudy went down the hall to examine Miss Dee. The bullet was lodged in the sheet.

"Homegirl got lucky," Ray Ray said, lighting up. The bullet had gone straight through her flesh. Ray Ray bandaged her too and then picked up the phone. He lit a cigarette and dialed 911.

"Come on. We better leave before they all come."

"No! Ray Ray, wait." Trudy held Ray Ray's arm. "I have to see about Vernita."

"Don't need to. I've already been there." Ray Ray looked down. He sucked in the smoke slow. "When she saw me she wouldn't talk. She just kept shaking her head. But Pearl showed up over there looking for you too. That's how I knew you were here."

"Tell me, Ray Ray!" Trudy said, worried. "Is Vernita okay?"

"Yeah, she'll make it, but she's hurt pretty bad. I stayed 'til the paramedics took her." Ray Ray looked over at Trudy's bandaged ear. "I hope all this bullshit was worth it."

Trudy looked at Ray Ray. His left eye was busted. He had bruise marks and welts all over his skin. A monstrous cut dissected his burn. Trudy held her head down. She'd never felt worse. She was responsible for everything that happened to her friends. All of them almost got killed. "If it wasn't for me, none of this would have happened."

* * *

Miss Dee looked at her bloody dead friend. Miss Dee stroked Agnes's head. Agnes had suffered. No one had been down to see her either. Loneliness had killed her a long time ago.

Trudy kept her head down. "I'm so sorry, Miss Dee. This was all my fault."

Miss Dee narrowed her eyes in worry.

Ray Ray smiled at Miss Dee while bandaging her leg. He whispered to Trudy, "We got to raise up, girl. Police'll be here in a minute."

Trudy cupped Miss Dee's face. "You gonna be all right?" She knew Ray Ray was right. They were fugitives now. She kissed Miss Dee's cheek. "See you, Miss Dee." She didn't have the heart to tell her she wouldn't be seeing her again.

Ray Ray and Trudy walked out the glass door. He lit a cigarette as they walked along the gravel road. The events of the last moments shook Trudy hard. A rush of tears streamed down her face.

"Dang," Trudy said, trying to stifle her crying, "you saved me, Ray Ray."

"Girl, you know I been had yo' back. I been telling you that shit forever." Ray Ray smiled and popped in a piece of Juicy Fruit gum. "I knew that stone fool would be coming after you. Vernita told me y'all was coming up here, so I figured I'd better come too." He winked back at Trudy and she managed a weak smile.

"We better raise up," Ray Ray said calmly. "Am-ba-lance and po-po be all over this place." They walked toward the Volkswagen. The highway was blazing. It raced with the hot, fast-paced traffic to Vegas.

Ray Ray blew out his smoke toward the loud, violent highway. He felt free next to Trudy under the million-starred sky. He pulled her mouth over his lips. Trudy didn't resist.

Ray Ray wrapped one arm around both of her shoulders, the other arm circling Trudy's waist. He felt a warm, luscious heat erupt from his stomach. He'd been waiting for this moment for a very long time. He squeezed Trudy real tight.

Suddenly, the Volkswagen roared back to life. Ray Ray ran over and jerked open the door.

Lil Steve looked at Trudy and then over at Ray Ray. A perplexed look passed over his face. But Lil Steve quickly masked any emotion he had. A grin eased its way across his fat, swollen jaw. "Zap-nin', people?" he said, trying to sound casual. He rubbed the groomed hairs on his chin.

Ray Ray was stunned. What was Lil Steve doing here? "Man, where you been? I've been waiting on you all night." He was talking loud over the Volkswagen's rattling engine while Lil Steve sat squeezing the wheel.

"What, you fixin' to raise?" Ray Ray wanted to know. "Where's all the muthafuckin' bank money, G?" Did Lil Steve rob him? Was homeboy trying to leave? Ray Ray waited for Lil Steve to speak.

Lil Steve's jaw was so bashed in, it killed him to talk, but Lil Steve had to tell him something. He could see it in Ray Ray's eyes. Ray Ray was about two snaps from going off, so Lil Steve decided to try to catch him off guard.

"You stealing my woman? What's up with that, man?" Lil Steve came out the car door.

Ray Ray immediately felt awkward standing so close to Trudy. He dropped his arm from her waist and took a few steps away. She was Lil Steve's ex. She was supposed to be off limits. He didn't know what else to say.

Trudy was just as nervous standing between them both. Because of her, both Ray Ray and Lil Steve were bleeding. All of them stood wondering who would speak first.

Lil Steve watched Trudy. He was glad he made her nervous. He walked up to Trudy and tried to slap her face but Ray Ray snatched back his hand.

"What's wrong with you, boy?" Lil Steve angrily said. "This bitch set us up! She played us both, Ray Ray! I know you didn't fall for her shit." Lil Steve tried to lunge at Trudy again but Ray Ray got between their bodies.

"Wait," Ray Ray said, holding Lil Steve back. "Be cool, man. There's no need to trip."

"Trip? Nigga, you the one trippin', cuz! I'm telling you, this bitch set us up!"

Ray Ray looked at Trudy but Trudy looked down.

"Tell him!" Lil Steve demanded. "Tell him how you got the money!"

Ray Ray eased his grip on Lil Steve's wrist.

"Man, she got the cash. She been playin' us all. She shot Charles and snatched up all the ends! He laying up in King Drew right now."

Ray Ray studied Lil Steve's face. Lil Steve was so adamant, so righteously pissed. He now knew Charles was shot, but Ray Ray didn't know by whom. Ray Ray looked back at Trudy again. Trudy wouldn't have crossed him. She wouldn't have set him up. She wouldn't do something that would send him back to prison. Trudy's dark eyes were glued to the ground. But maybe she would. He'd been gone for almost two years. Maybe she and Lil Steve used him all along. Maybe he was the one playing the fool. But then he remembered what Charles had said about the money.

"Naw, man, you wrong," Ray Ray said calmly. He spoke soft and slow, like he was sorting things together. "Charles got the money by selling Flo's car." Ray Ray waited for Trudy, expecting validation, but Trudy kept her eyes on the ground.

"Oh, wow. Come on, man, she's clowning you, dog. Charles didn't sell shit. Think about it, homie. Why the fuck would some drug dealer be tryin' to off us, huh? Where's our money from the bank? I bet we didn't get jack. I'm telling you this bitch set us up from day one."

Ray Ray looked confused. He didn't know what to say. It was true, his blue envelope only held newspaper shreds. He turned from Lil Steve and completely faced Trudy.

Trudy grabbed Ray Ray's arm. She tried to hold Ray Ray's hand.

"I told you don't do it, Ray Ray. I begged you, remember?" Trudy's pleading eyes tried to make Ray Ray understand.

Ray Ray pulled his arm away. He stared at her hard. She ground her right foot in the sand.

"See, man! I'm telling you she played you, my brotha. Didn't I say from day one she was foul."

"He's lying to you, Ray Ray. He's always lied to you about me."

Ray Ray backed away. He looked Trudy up and down. All he knew was that it was really getting hard not to smash one of these fools in the ground.

"She's been using you, Ray Ray. Selling you wolf tickets, homes. Your dick got your vision all twisted."

Ray Ray pushed past them both. He didn't want to listen to this madness. Though he couldn't hear them yet and they were miles away, Ray Ray could faintly see the flashing red and blue lights of the cops.

Trudy grabbed his hand and gently turned him around.

"Remember that party?" she asked. "The first time we ever spent together."

Ray Ray looked down. He bit his lower lip. It was the night he went to jail. Before he and Lil Steve did that robbery. "I try my best to erase it."

"Don't listen to her bullshit, man. All women lie. Lyin' and bitches is like dog shit and flies," Lil Steve said.

Trudy ignored Lil Steve and kept her focus on Ray Ray. "I felt something that night. I know you felt something too."

Ray Ray remembered that evening full well. Though he never spoke about it once, the memory loomed in his mind. In prison, he'd played it back hundreds of times. He used to lie on his cot and think about it for hours. With his eyes closed he could still see what Trudy had on. An ivory lace dress, with thin skinny straps, her hair piled high on her head. He remembered how good it felt to touch her. The rich brown warmth of her skin. But in a fraction of a second the whole thing was over. Next thing he knew he was stuck doing time and Trudy was with Lil Steve.

Lil Steve disgustedly spit on the ground. "Who gives a fuck 'bout some damn high school party! We talking about how we got pimped up here, G! We talking 'bout how this nasty trick dogged us!" Lil Steve turned to Trudy and got in her face. "Don't cloud it by bringing up that janky shit now!" Lil Steve didn't want Trudy to talk about the party.

"This 'ho got your nose blown open so wide

you couldn't see this raggedy shit coming." Lil Steve stared at Ray Ray. He shook his head, disgusted. "She's working you, man, just like she worked Charles, and that nigga's laying in King Drew barely breathing." Lil Steve sneered in Trudy's fuming face.

But Trudy stepped up to Lil Steve this time. She whipped back her braids, putting one hand on her hip.

"You don't want me to tell him, huh? Look, you're scared as shit now. You're scared I'ma tell what really happened that night!" Trudy said.

But Lil Steve ignored her. He turned his back on her face. He laughed, leaning against Ray Ray's shoulder, rubbing his slender goatee. "Ain't this a bitch. She's trying to flip the script, man. She stuck Charles, dog. Shot him point-blank. Now she wants to tell some fairy tale shit about the past. I'm telling you, you're dealing with a garden tool, man. She ain't nothing but a cold-blooded 'ho!"

The cops were almost there, but suddenly they wildly veered off when they got a call that a drunk driver had hit the center divide.

"Go ahead, call me names," Trudy said boldly. "But I'm still gonna tell him what happened."

"Come on, man. Am I making this up? This bitch is just like her tired-ass mama," Lil Steve said.

Trudy ignored him. She wiped her braids back. "Yeah, I'm like Mama. We both got a few

263

flaws but Mama could always recognize bullshit when she saw it. Your name-calling is not gonna stop me from talking. I'm telling this shit whether you like it or not." Trudy whirled around and faced Ray Ray full on.

"That night at the party, Lil Steve was watching us, I remember. I thought he looked worried. I was wondering why he kept staring. Next thing I know he starts blowing me kisses, licking his thin, nasty lips."

"That's a lie! I didn't even go to that party."

But Ray Ray remembered. Lil Steve definitely was there.

"First, I ignored him. Refused to look his way. But when you left to get a drink, Lil Steve came over. He told me you were high. He said he'd been listening. He said everything you told me that night was fiction and that you were nothing but a heroin addict who served time."

"That's a lie! I never said that!" Lil Steve wanted to slap Trudy's face.

Ray Ray looked at Lil Steve but decided to stay silent. He wanted to hear the rest of what Trudy had to say.

"He said y'all had business. Said you had to do some job and he'd be damned if he let some young trick like me mess it up. I thought he was crazy. I told him to leave. But Lil Steve just stood there and played with his mustache. I tried to push past him but he blocked my way. 'I'ma take you,' Lil Steve told me. 'Watch how I work it,' he said. 'Ray Ray won't never know what happened.'"

Ray Ray raised both his eyebrows but still he said nothing.

"Don't listen to this tramp. Can't you see she's crazy? Look at her, man. She ain't even fine. You seen my stable. None of my 'hos look like her." Lil Steve thought insulting her would make Trudy stop. But Trudy was already on a roll.

"What I remember," Ray Ray glanced at Trudy as he spoke, "is that I went to jail and then got sent to prison. When I came back you'd already been with my man."

Lil Steve smiled. "Yeah, I fucked her. So what? So had every other damn dick in town."

"He lied to you, Ray Ray! But you couldn't see. Lil Steve's been manipulating your ass from day one. And you walk around with your dumb little codes. Not talking to his girl. Shit, he didn't give a fuck! He didn't want me. He's always been selfish. He didn't want you near me because he wanted you to do that job. He wanted to use you so he could get some money, and you're the one who ended up doing time."

"Shut up!" Lil Steve screamed. "You fuckin' got damn slut!"

"Lil Steve was my first," Trudy said to Ray Ray. "I was a virgin and Lil Steve knew it."

Ray Ray could not believe what Trudy was saying. A virgin. That's not what he'd heard.

265

"She's a liar!" Lil Steve screamed. "That ain't how it went down!"

"He knew if you had someone decent in your life, you'd see him for the crackhead he is."

Lil Steve lunged at Trudy. "I ain't no crack-head, you bitch!"

But Ray Ray remembered. He had lots of time to think in prison. Lil Steve told him Trudy was no good. He'd told him everyone at that party had already had her. That she'd been with a whole bunch of men. But Ray Ray never heard that from anyone else. All Lil Steve kept saying was that he shouldn't trust no woman and that the only thing trustworthy was money.

"You listened to him and you ended up in jail!" Trudy said.

Ray Ray recalled the robbery. Lil Steve stayed in the car. He told Ray Ray he'd drive and would wait by the curb. But the liquor store had a security camera. They arrested Ray Ray and Lil Steve got away. And Ray Ray never ratted on his friend. He looked at Trudy again. Some of what she said made sense but he knew she had a part in this too.

"Well, you ended up with blood. You must have wanted him too." Ray Ray lit one of Jimmy's cigars and blew his smoke down the long dusty road.

"They put you away for close to two years, Ray Ray. Lil Steve kept coming. Kept sniffing at my door. He told me you didn't want me and that you were locked in there for life."

Ray Ray was pissed. "What difference does it make?" He tossed his lit butt down the long, littered highway.

"That's right, dog! None of that shit has to do with the bank. Yeah, I had her. So what? Shit, I had lots of women. It's not like the shit was a secret." Lil Steve spit down on the asphalt again. "The bottom line is this trick set us up. Keep yo' ass focused on that!"

"I set *you* up, punk! You dumb muthafucker! You made Ray Ray come, just like you did last time. You always make him do your dirty work for you, while you always hide in the car!"

Ray Ray asked Trudy point-blank, "So what is it, shorty? You did this bank shit with Charles?"

The way Ray Ray said "shorty" was like he separated himself from her now, like she didn't mean more than some chick on the street.

"Wait, Ray Ray, listen. Lil Steve got it twisted. Charles did help me out. But I didn't shoot him. Flo shot him because she thought me and Charles were messing around."

"Were you?" Ray Ray asked. He'd seen Trudy and Charles together a couple times. He didn't know which part was true.

"Hell, yeah, she was. I'm telling you she's scandalous! I saw 'em sneak away a whole gang of times. Creeping off after the show."

"Why are you lying on me, Lil Steve? What did I ever do to you?"

Lil Steve almost smiled. She really was cute. "Do to me? Ain't that a muthafuckin' blip. You used me and Ray Ray to take the fall for this job." He had Trudy against the ropes. There was nowhere for her to go, and he could see his boy Ray Ray was bending toward him.

"Something musta happened." Lil Steve sneered. "Nobody just comes after your ass with a gun. Yo' big ass musta done something."

Trudy saw the doubt entering inside Ray Ray's eyes. She ignored Lil Steve and tried to talk just to Ray Ray. She had to make him understand. "Look, Ray Ray, I did do the bank job with Charles. I tried to tell you that day but you just got out from prison. I didn't want to get you involved in a crime. I wanted to protect you. I wanted you to stay clean. But Lil Steve sucked you back in. I'm sorry. I didn't think it would turn out like this. All I wanted to do was pay his ass back and get the fuck out of L.A.!" Trudy tried to hold Ray Ray's hand but he moved.

Trudy stepped to Lil Steve. She got in his face. "Why don't you tell him about that videotape, huh? Same kind of videotape you made of me. Tell him how you finked on your friend."

Lil Steve swung at Trudy, but Ray Ray blocked his arm.

"He was so proud. He couldn't resist telling. Always talking about Teflon! How he's never been caught. He did get caught and would have definitely done time, but they let him go because he gave you up!"

"How the fuck would you know? You weren't even there." Lil Steve looked at Trudy with a confident air. He tried to leap toward her again but she moved farther away, backing up toward the highway. They were all standing right near the traffic.

" 'Cause you told! Vernita told me you bragged to her about it. Said it was business. That you had to give Ray Ray up. That you weren't going to jail no matter what," Trudy said.

See, that night, after the robbery, they picked Lil Steve up too. They kept him in a room asking him questions for hours. They played him the videotape again and again. The video showed a bandana-faced man holding a gun, running toward the liquor store door. It was Ray Ray but the cops didn't know it at the time. All they knew is they had Lil Steve. The cops worked a special deal for giving Ray Ray up. Ray Ray went upstate, got a year and a half at Norco. Lil Steve got a slap on the wrist.

Ray Ray was stunned. Was this really true? All this time he figured the storeowner was the one who popped him. He couldn't believe it was really Lil Steve. Maybe that's why they nabbed him so fast. Ray Ray looked at Lil Steve hard. He couldn't believe what he was hearing but deep down he knew it was true.

Lil Steve noticed the heat in Ray Ray's eyes, so he tried to quickly shift the blame to Trudy.

"She set us up, man," Lil Steve said fast. "Look all around you. Homeboy lying over there is shot. She dealt with that brotha. Charles is laying up bloody, that's another brotha she had, and we don't want to mention what happened to Vernita and that was her own got damn friend!" Lil Steve steeled himself when he said that last part. It was hard to lie about what had happened to Vernita. He felt guilty but he knew how to bury it well. "She fucked over us, man. That's a muthafuckin' fact. Ain't no two ways about that!"

"Ray Ray, I did pull this job," Trudy said, coming clean. "I didn't want you involved. I did try to stop you, but I didn't know nothing about taking that cocaine."

Hearing the word "cocaine" immediately triggered something inside Lil Steve. He looked at the cocaine bag in the paneling of the car. His mouth started to water. The cocaine called his name. He could see the loose duct tape flapping in the wind. He wiped his dry lips before speaking. "Don't trust a big butt and a smile," Lil Steve said. "They even make songs about raw chicks like her."

In the distance, there was the faint driving sound of sirens. The cops were trying to get the drunk driver to pull over.

Lil Steve inched close to Ray Ray. He stood right in front of his face.

"Man, this bitch gonna send yo' ass back to the pen. 5-0 is coming. We got to raise up. Let's off her ass and get in the car!"

Trudy looked horrified. What was Lil Steve saying? A second ago, Ray Ray had just saved her life. Now Lil Steve was trying to tell him to kill her.

"Come on, man. It's just you and me, homes. Get this shit over with once and for all and let's go sip some mai tais and see some titties on the Strip."

Ray Ray hesitated. He didn't want to shoot Trudy. He still couldn't believe his good friend had turned him in.

Lil Steve leaned closer to Ray Ray's suit jacket.

At that range Ray Ray noticed a powdery substance faintly sprinkled over his mustache. Lil Steve was definitely high.

Lil Steve felt the cocaine kicking in full steam. He'd snorted a whole lot while Ray Ray and Trudy were inside but now his body was aching for more. Lil Steve's arm started to mildly shake. Sweat leaked down his long, narrow back.

But before Ray Ray knew it, Lil Steve grabbed Ray Ray's gun from the underarm holster and pointed it at Trudy's head.

Ray Ray tried to reach for it but Lil Steve backed up.

"Get away from me, man. I'm not playing with you no more. I'm haveta put your work in myself."

"Dog, what are you doing?" Ray Ray said fast. "You ain't got to kill her. Let's just split the shit and go." Ray Ray tried to lunge toward Lil Steve's arm but Lil Steve jerked back. He raised the gun to Ray Ray's chest.

"Don't fuck with me, man. This ain't about you, dog." Lil Steve stared at the cocaine inside the car, then he stared back at Trudy. His tongue drew a line across his top lip. He wanted to kill Trudy, but he wanted that coke too.

He made Ray Ray take a step back. He got in and revved the VW engine. He pointed the gun back at Trudy. "I got business with this trick. Stay out of it, dog."

"Homegirl's always been my business," Ray Ray said loudly over the sound of the engine. He stood right in front of Trudy's body.

"She ain't worth it, man. Move over, G!" Lil Steve's hand shook while holding the gun. Sweat dripped down from his face.

"Naw, man. I can't let you go out like this, dog."

"She ain't shit. Don't let no tramp come between friends." Lil Steve pointed his gun at Ray Ray's scarred face. "Look what the last 'ho did to your mug. You better step off this bitch, homes."

But Ray Ray just stood there. He wouldn't

move over. Car after car was whizzing by them now. The wind blew some sand into his eyes.

"She got you so whipped and your ass only smelled it. You tripping and you ain't even had you a taste." Lil Steve pulled back the safety on Ray Ray's large gun. "Sorry, dude, but I have to do this." His finger rolled over the trigger.

Suddenly, a red sports car came zigzagging up. The car came so close it whipped the gun from Lil Steve's hand. The gun danced across the thick double lines. Lil Steve was stunned. He turned his back to the highway. A semi was coming down the hill the opposite way. But the weaving red sports car made the truck driver brake hard. Lil Steve tried to get the VW Bug into gear but was shaking and couldn't find the right groove. The driver tried his best to keep the Mack truck in line. But the red car came so close, the truck driver had to swerve, forcing the semi to jackknife.

Ray Ray and Trudy raced out of the way. But Lil Steve was in the Bug. He struggled to get it going. The Mack driver honked the horn a long time. He lost control and hoped the Bug would move out of the way. But it was no use; he was coming too fast. He smacked the Volkswagen like it was a gnat. The hubcaps flew off. Smoke rose from the tires. The truck dragged the car over five hundred yards before the crumpled thing fell off the grill. The Bug was completely engulfed in dark smoke. The desert black night blazed with tall orangey flames. The red car kept going. It never eased its pace. Its taillights melted toward the gambling lights of the state line.

Ray Ray ran to the Volkswagen but couldn't get past the fire. He looked down the highway and saw a trail of approaching lights. The ambulance roared. The police sirens grew louder.

You could see Lil Steve struggling wildly with the driver's door. He was screaming and mouthing the word "help." Ray Ray ran into the fire. Ran straight through the flames but he couldn't open the Bug's smashed-in door. Lil Steve was frantic. He couldn't get out. His horrible screams didn't sound human. He was trying to open the door with one hand. The other clutched the cocaine and money.

Trudy yelled out, "Hurry up, Ray Ray! The police are almost here!"

The sirens grew louder. You could see the cars now. In a moment they would be at the scene.

Ray Ray struggled and pulled, but the front door was stuck. He ran from the flames. His clothing was scorched. He bent down and put both his hands on his knees. He struggled to catch his own breath. When he darted through the flames again he just came back choking.

"Ray Ray, come on!" Trudy said, worried about the fire. "Get away from there. It could explode!"

But he couldn't leave his friend burning up like that. He ran back but this time went to the passenger's side and pulled the door open wide.

Ray Ray noticed an oily trail leaking out from the tank. It was headed for the hungry red flames. Ray Ray was coughing hysterically now. The smoke fumes had ripped through his lungs. Lil Steve was passed out. The carbon monoxide got him. But Ray Ray was determined. He wanted to save his friend. So as the fire burned his skin, Ray Ray went all the way in and yanked Lil Steve away from the car.

He dragged Lil Steve away from the flames. Lil Steve's left leg was smoking and charred. One shoe was gone. His foot was burnt black. His pants leg had melted into his skin. Ray Ray started to drag Lil Steve farther out, but Lil Steve screamed out in pain.

"Leave him," Trudy said.

Ray Ray flashed her cold eyes.

"No, Ray Ray, look, you don't understand. If we take him with us he'll never survive the trip. We got two solid hours before we hit Vegas. If the ambulance takes him he still has a chance. But we gotta go now!"

Ray Ray and Trudy raced to Tony's black Caddy. Ray Ray revved the V8 and floored the gas pedal hard. In a second the cops had circled the scene. Trudy and Ray Ray were less than eighty feet away. But Ray Ray kept the lights off. Luckily the Caddy was black and there was a whole lot of smoke. It was easy to fade into the night.

Ray Ray looked in his rearviews at the wild flaming sky. The paramedics put Lil Steve on a stretcher.

Suddenly the Volkswagen blew up like a bomb. Shards of hot metal shot toward the sky. A fireball rose from the ground.

"Dayam," Ray Ray said looking at the flames. Trudy looked back and then fell against his shoulder. She felt like a wet sack of dirt.

Trudy's eyes followed the smoke to the sky.

"I'm sorry. I'm so sorry. This whole thing's my fault."

Ray Ray touched her cheek. He gently rubbed her back.

Trudy wept in her hands. She couldn't look again. Hot tears raced down from her eyes. That life was over. She couldn't go home again. But now she had no reason to keep going ahead.

Ray Ray wiped her face with the hem of his shirt.

His own eyes trailed down the dark two-way road. His brain went a million miles per hour.

They drove in cold silence for over two hours. Trudy couldn't look at Ray Ray. She just felt too bad, so she kept her head tilted toward her window instead. She only looked at Ray Ray in her peripheral vision. He was gripping the steering wheel tight.

Trudy couldn't take the silence and finally faced him full on. She wrung both her hands in her lap. "Ray Ray, I swear, I was telling the truth."

Ray Ray didn't speak. He kept looking straight ahead. Then he swerved the car over into the right lane and rolled into a rest area. He kept holding the wheel, staring straight at the trees. Finally Ray Ray turned to her and spoke.

"Listen. Prison gave me a whole lot of time to reflect. I knew Lil Steve worked something but I never was sure. That's what made doing my time seem so hard. Lil Steve was my boy. Me and him always been friends. We been hanging out in the streets since day one. When my brother died, Lil Steve was the only one I had left. I didn't want to fuck that shit up."

"I'm the one who fucked everything up," Trudy said. "I created all this mess and we still don't have jack." Trudy covered her face and just bawled.

Ray Ray pulled a stuffed pillowcase out from the backseat. He placed the large sack in her lap. There was stack after stack of thick wads of hundreds, wad after wad of fifties and twenties, all held by fat rubber bands.

"Where'd you get all this? This is not from the bank." Trudy stared at the cash in complete disbelief.

Ray Ray didn't say this money came from Tony. He shifted the Caddy from Park and the tires ate the gravel. But he stopped before swinging the car back to the highway and pressing his foot on the gas.

"This is Ray Ray, remember. I still got skills, baby." Ray Ray smiled, letting his eyes leave the road for a moment. He rubbed his cross and tooled the car toward the bright Vegas lights. "But I'm ready to go legit, if you let me."

Ray Ray grabbed Trudy's body and squeezed her firm skin. He held her like he'd wanted to hold her for years. He kissed her long and hard, smothering her face and neck, tears brimming inside his eyes. His sincerity shocked her. She'd never felt so alive. She kissed Ray Ray like she had wanted to do that first night. Like there was nothing else she wanted more in life.

25

Flo and Charles

Now, most folks would have thought that after someone done shot ya, you'd never speak to their sorry ass ever in life. Not so with Charles and Flo. Soon as he got better he was back at the house. Screaming and fussing right where they left off. Cussing and saying stuff like "I never touched her." And Flo screaming back that she saw him. Round and around. Over and over. Oh, those fools fussed, cried and carried on so. Breaking things. Ripping stuff up like old sheets. Taking some of them fights to the street! But they stayed together. Never busted up. Bandages, bad feeling and all. Charles spent most of his time looking out of the window, wondering if one day she might show.

People talked about Trudy like she was some kind of legend. Gangbangers tagged the city with Ray Ray's face and name. Nobody they knew ever robbed them a bank. Or ever left a drug dealer to die in the desert. Beauty shops yakked, men in bars wondered. Folks who never spoke kindly to Trudy in life said that she was their very dear friend. Vernita was the only one who knew the whole truth. But she didn't see many of those folks anymore since she opened her new salon in Oakland.

Lil Steve lied to anyone who gave him a listen. He lost the use of his leg and was in a wheelchair now. Told everyone he saw that he'd thought of it all. That the bank plan was his invention. But most folks shook their heads and kept walking past. Only crackheads and drunks paid him any attention. If he was the big mastermind of it all, why did he live in that smelly flophouse up the block? Pearl would watch him outside from Dee's Parlor sometimes, his one leg just as thin as a golf club. Sometimes he came in for a short stack or coffee and Pearl never charged him a dime. Dee's Parlor was a maple-smelling breakfast place now. Miss Dee lived there again and Pearl helped her run it, and at two ninety-nine for pancakes, grits and eggs, they were packed every day of the week. They even delivered food to shut-ins, like Ray Ray's mother, who now lived in a roomy apartment in View Park. Joan came once, turned her nose up at the place, then disappeared for a few weeks. She didn't answer her phone, didn't come out of the house and never told a soul that Mr. Hall left her. You just didn't see Joan around anymore. Pearl walked on over one day. Joan's Mercedes was there but when she called out her name, nobody came to the door, so she jimmied the lock and went in. She found Joan facedown with the oven turned on. Her bun was undone and her gray had grown out. She died with her face on the rack. She was clutching a tiny white sheet in her hand. It was a large Western Union check from Trudy.

See, a Western Union man showed up out of the blue once. He handed out checks to Pearl and Vernita. There was no return address or mention from whom.

Nobody, not one soul in the bucket of blood town ever heard from Trudy or Ray Ray again.

It's funny how you can want something so bad you can taste it. In your brain you can feel the thing touching your hand. Like if you don't get it now your whole arm might fall off. You can stretch but it always seems to keep out of reach. But wanting is like gnawing away at a flea or a howling dog scratching away at the screen. Sooner or later it just don't itch as much, or you just go someplace and lay down. And the next thing you know, a few months will go by and that feeling, that hot need, is a memory now and all of that wanting is gone.

Flo sat on the couch and quietly rolled up her hair, while their small baby napped on her thighs. Charles walked to the sink and drank his cold beer alone. It was March and already feeling like summer. Charles stared out the window a really long time. His eyes never left the hot scene beyond the screen. He scratched at his neck while swallowing slow. He licked his chapped lips and grinned toward the glass, as the big-legged girl across the street mowed her lawn.

The most lethal ride-or-die women in Memphis now run their gangs and the streets. But the aftermath of an all-out war means merciless new enemies, time-bomb secrets . . . and one chance to take it all . . .

BOSS DIVAS

Available September 2014 wherever books and ebooks are sold.

1

Ta'Shara

"STOP THE FUCKING CAR!"

Profit slams on the brakes while I bolt out of the passenger car door and race into the night toward my foster parents' burning house.

"TRACEE! REGGIE!" *They're not in there. Please, God. Don't let them be in there.* "TRACEE! REGGIE!"

"Ta'Shara, wait up," Profit yells. His long strides eat up the distance between us even as I shove my way through the city's emergency responders. I've never seen flames stretch so high or felt such intense heat. Still, none of that shit stopped me. In my delusional mind, there is still time to get them out of there.

"Hey, lady. You can't go in there," someone shouts and makes a grab for me.

As I draw closer to the front porch, Profit is

able to wrap one of his powerful arms around my waist and lift me off my feet. "Baby, stop. You can't go in there."

"Let me go!" My legs pedal in the air as I stretch uselessly for the door. "TRACEE! REGGIE!" My screams rake my throat raw.

Profit drags me away from the growing flames.

Men in uniform rush over to us. I don't know who they are and I don't care. I just need to know one thing. "Where are my parents? Did they make it out?"

"Ma'am, calm down. Please tell me your name."

"WHERE ARE THEY?"

"Ma'am—"

"ANSWER ME, DAMMIT!"

"C'mon, man," Profit says. "Give my girl something."

The fireman draws a deep breath and then drops a bomb that changes my life forever.

"The neighbors reported the fire. Right now, I'm not aware of anyone making it out of the house. I'm sorry."

"NOOOOOOO!" I collapse in Profit's arm. He hauls me up against his six-three frame and I lay my head on his broad chest. Before, I found comfort in his strong embrace, but not tonight. I sob uncontrollably as pain overwhelms me, but then I make out a familiar car down the street.

"Oh. My. God."

Profit tenses. "What?"

My eyes aren't deceiving me. Sitting behind the wheel of her burgundy Crown Victoria is LeShelle, with a slow smile creeping across her face. She forms a gun with her hand and pretends to fire at us.

We're next.

LeShelle tosses back her head and, despite the siren's wail, the roaring fire, and the chaos around me, that bitch's maniacal laugh rings in my ears.

How much more of this shit am I going to take? When will this fuckin' bullshit end?

BOOM!

The crowd gasps while windows explode from the top floor of the house, but my gaze never waivers from LeShelle. My tears dry up as anger grips me.

She did this shit. I don't need a jury to tell me that the bitch is guilty as hell. How long has she been threatening the Douglases' lives? Why in the hell didn't I believe that she would follow through?

LeShelle has proven her ruthlessness time after time. This fucking Gangster Disciples versus the Vice Lords shit ain't a game to her. It's a way of life. And she doesn't give a fuck who she hurts.

My blood boils and all at once everything

burst out of me. I wrench away from Profit's protective arms and take off toward LeShelle in a rage.

"I'M GOING TO FUCKING KILL YOU!"

"TA'SHARA, NO!" Profit shouts.

I ignore him as I race toward LeShelle's car. My hot tears burn tracks down my face.

LeShelle laughs in my face and then pulls off from the curb, but not before I'm able to pound my fist against the trunk.

Profit's arms wrap back around my waist, but I kick out and connect with LeShelle's taillight and shatter that mutherfucka. The small wave of satisfaction I get is quickly erased when her piece of shit car burps out a black cloud of exhaust in my face.

"NO! Don't let her get away. No!"

"Ta'Shara, please. Not now. Let it go!"

Let it go? I round on Profit. "How the fuck can you say that shit?"

BOOM!

More windows explode, drawing my attention back to the only place that I've ever called home. My heart claws its way out of my chest as orange flames and black smoke lick the sky.

My legs give out and my knees kiss the concrete, all the while Profit's arms remain locked around me. I can't hear what he's saying because my sobs drown him out.

"This is all my fault," tumbles over my tongue.

I conjure up an image of Tracee and Reggie: the last time I'd seen them. It's a horrible memory. Everyone was angry and everyone said things that…they can never be taken back.

Grief consumes me. I squeeze my eyes tight and cling to the ghosts inside of my head. "I'm sorry. I'm so sorry."

Profit's arms tighten. I melt in his arms even though I want to lash out. *Isn't it his fault for my foster parents roasting in that house, too?* When the question crosses my mind I crumble from the weight of my shame.

I'm to blame. No one else.

A heap in the center of the street, I lay my head against Profit's chest again and take in the horrific sight through a steady sheen of tears. The Douglases were good people. All they wanted was the best for me and for me to believe in myself. They would've done the same for LeShelle if she'd given them the chance.

LeShelle fell in love with the streets and the make-believe power of being the head bitch of the Queen Gs. I didn't want anything to do with any of that bullshit, but it didn't matter. I'm viewed as GD property by blood, and the shit hit the fan when I fell in love with Profit—a Vice Lord by blood. Back then Profit wasn't a soldier yet. But our being together was taken as a sign of disrespect. LeShelle couldn't let it slide.

However, the harder I fight the streets' politics, the more I'm dragged down into her bull-shit world of gangs and violence.

"I should have killed her when I had the chance." If I had Tracee and Reggie would still be alive. "She won't get away with this," I vow. "I'm going to kill her if it's the last thing I do."

The Hottest African American Fiction
from
Dafina Books

Sizzling Fiction from
Dafina Books